CHANCE

What Reviewers Say About The Author

"Fulton has rescued the romance from formulaic complacency by asking universal questions about friendship and love, intimacy and lust. The answers reflect both depth and maturity; this is the romance novel grown up a bit. Girl gets girl is always popular; more inspirational is when the girl gets to know herself."—*The Lesbian Review of Books*

"Fulton takes an age old formula for love and plants it in modern surroundings. The writing is smart and quick, and she portrays innocence with loving, irresistible humor. She delivers flesh-warming, flush-inducing seduction and pages of slippery, richly textured sex. Her knack for depicting current social dilemmas also makes her a compelling contemporary author."—*The Lesbian Review of Books*

"Fulton has penned another wonderfully readable, erotically-charged book...fun, and well worth your time."—*Lambda Book Report*

"Fulton tells a dark and disturbing tale of friendship and betrayal, of love lost before it has a chance to begin. That may sound rather hackneyed but her use of these themes is anything but trite. The writing is outstanding...Fulton creates characters that live on in the memory and in the heart...An extraordinary novel. I could not put it down and days later, I'm still thinking about it."—*Bay Area Reporter*

"Perhaps needless to say, the paths the friendships take are fraught with, among other things, lust, unrequited love, infidelity and dishonesty. Good intentions are trampled in the pursuit of passion. Problems, both past and present, shape the relationships the women share....The writing is sharp...a realistic account of contemporary urban lesbian life."—*Melbourne Star Observer*

"The ending left me grinning to myself for hours and wishing for an immediately available sequel... One of the best writers on the roster.... Her books are always entertaining and often thought provoking."—*Dimensions*

"I'm not sure why I found the book so completely erotic. The author knows how to tease and how to deliver."—*Lesbiana*

"One of those books that is hard to put down until you finish it... Whether you're in the perfect relationship or still looking for it, you'll enjoy this story."—*MegaScene*

CHANCE

by
Jennifer Fulton writing as
GRACE LENNOX

2006

CHANCE

ISBN 1-933110-31-7

THIS TRADE PAPERBACK ORIGINAL IS PUBLISHED BY
BOLD STROKES BOOKS, INC.,
PENNSYLVANIA, USA

FIRST PRINTING: BOLD STROKES BOOKS 2006

CREDITS
EDITOR: STACIA SEAMAN
PRODUCTION DESIGN: STACIA SEAMAN
COVER DESIGN BY SHERI (GRAPHICARTIST2020@HOTMAIL.COM)

By the Author

MYSTERIES as Rose Beecham

Amanda Valentine Series

Introducing Amanda Valentine

Second Guess

Fair Play

Jude Devine Series

Grave Silence

ROMANCES as Jennifer Fulton

Moon Island Series

A Guarded Heart

Passion Bay

Saving Grace

The Sacred Shore

Heartstoppers Series

Dark Dreamer

Others

Greener Than Grass

True Love

Acknowledgments

I could not do the job I love without the support and encouragement of my long-suffering family and friends, especially my partner, Fel. My daughter Sophie provided invaluable information and insight as I wrote this story, and Stacia Seaman, as always, edited with care and precision. Finally, I thank Radclyffe for her writerly insights and her friendship, and for making this business fun.

Dedication

For Sophie.

Beloved daughter, you are the best thing I ever did.

CHAPTER ONE

When I was ten, a fortune-teller read my palm. Actually, it was my Aunt Shirley. She went through a clairvoyant phase before she became an evangelical Christian. Nowadays, she attributes her crystal ball predictions to Satan, probably because most of them came true. For example, my parents got a divorce when I was thirteen, just like Aunt Shirley said. A year later my father, who was certainly enslaved by the devil during his male menopause, married a former Miss California. They kept her sash, crown, and stilettos enshrined in a revolving glass showcase in their living room.

The divorce was how Mom and I ended up living with my grandparents in a small Northern California town called Eureka. There, in the hills, Mom sold real estate to San Francisco executives who wanted to live an alternative lifestyle, while I spent each summer vacation chasing girls who would not have me.

Eventually, when I was twenty, Dad came to his senses and divorced the beauty queen and he and Mom got back together after going to Hawaii on a tantric retreat. The divorce settlement left the beauty queen in possession of our house and Dad poor, but Mom didn't care. She was a big success by then, thanks to her copious real estate development deals in Silicon Valley. These days my parents run a meditation and enrichment center in Sausalito called Beyond Limits, which, according to my best friend, Suzie Weissmuller, is what happens to your credit card when you go there.

As well as predicting family crises, my Aunt Shirley told me I was destined to encounter true love amidst depravity and loud music. I spent years hanging out at dances and clubs hoping for the Big Moment, and to tell you the truth, I had just gotten to thinking it would never happen when I found myself sinking Buds with Suzie in the Lexington one September evening and—gasp! There she was.

Short dark hair. 501s. Black turtleneck. Leather jacket. She owned the room the moment she set foot in the door. Everyone stared. She seemed oblivious.

"Wow," I choked. "Check it out."

Suzie glanced up from her drink. "Where?"

The divine stranger sauntered to the bar like she had a patent on the satisfaction gene. One tiny thick gold earring clung to her left earlobe. I imagined she smelled of salt air and gasoline, fresh from cruising the city in a hot convertible.

"Omigod, she's looking at us." I was ready to take a dive off the Golden Gate Bridge if she offered to watch.

"Get a hold of yourself," Suzie said and waved at the goddess.

I nearly ate my beer glass. "You know her?"

She was coming toward us, one thumb tucked in her hip pocket. I had never seen anything so sexy. I prayed she was not another one of Suzie's exes.

Suzie got up and planted a kiss right on the stranger's mouth. I could feel the room receding as if everyone and everything in it had been swallowed by fog. A pair of arresting midnight blue eyes found mine. I stood up. My chair overbalanced and hit the floor.

"Chance…" Suzie said, "meet Eric."

Eric? I nearly whimpered. *No. It could not be true.*

"Chance was kind of hoping you were a girl," Suzie explained.

"So was my mother." The voice was bedroom pitched.

I picked up my chair and sat down again, all set to weep into my beer. "Do you make a habit of drinking in lesbian bars?" I asked the sex-goddess impersonator.

He rolled a cigarette, then offered his tobacco and papers around. "I'm on the run from fag hags," he said. "They're too scared to come in here with Pagan on the door."

I glanced across a sea of jostling bodies to the six-foot muscle machine carding young things at the door. Pagan was the lesbian Terminator, only minus the humor. I'd heard she once turned down security on Monica Lewinsky because it could damage her reputation. Pagan's, that was.

Suzie constructed a cigarette like a joint, compressing each end to secure the contents. "Thank God lesbians never have to deal with the fag hag trip," she said. "I mean, can you imagine a bunch of giggling straight men hanging off your every word and wanting to watch you try on clothes at the mall?"

Eric smirked. "I think about that all the time."

For a moment I wondered if I'd been conned. He couldn't be a boy. Those smoky blue-black eyes surely belonged to the woman of my dreams. He caught me looking and glanced down at my newspaper. I covered the personals with my hand but it was too late.

"Scored recently?" he inquired.

The red circles I'd made in the *Girl Wants Girl* columns stuck out like warts on a supermodel's butt. I forced casual laughter. "I never get 'round to writing anyway."

Suzie fingered an ad. "This one sounds interesting. 'Independent mature lesbian seeks cute energetic young woman to spoil.'"

"Read between *those* lines," I said, scornful. I was not looking for a sugar mama.

"Or this one." Suzie wasn't letting up. "'She broke my heart and took my cat, but I still have my pride…'"

"It's a country song." Eric improvised a few bars.

He could sing in tune. My misery was complete. The women around us stared. I wasn't the only lonely heart he'd fooled.

"He's not transgender, is he?" I whispered into Suzie's ear.

"Ask him," she said.

I was too embarrassed. "Got any sisters?" I inquired hopefully.

Eric shook his head. "I wish."

On principle I did not want to like him, but there was something disarming about Eric, a wry self-mockery that made freezing him out difficult. Any negative I tried to see in him seemed a petty consequence of my disappointment, or worse—some deep-seated insecurity.

Suzie was scanning the talent. "Look. Over there in the plaid mini, kissing the biker. She's cute."

"If you want a spare tongue," Eric said.

I shrugged. "She's not my type. Too young."

"Is it just sex you're after?" Eric asked.

"No. She wants the works," Suzie responded on my behalf. "Flowers, courtship…"

"Friendship is what's really important to me," I said. It sounded like the lie that it was. The affirmations weren't working.

"What happened to that babe with the dog?" Suzie asked.

Last month's disaster. "We weren't even doing anything, but it kept staring and growling…"

"Don't you hate that?" Eric said.

"I once had this lover who had a rat." Suzie launched into one of her show-stopper anecdotes. "She was a firefighter."

"Please," I groaned. "Not the rat story."

Such was my life. Twenty-six. Single. Going nowhere. By now you are probably thinking: *what's wrong with her?* I used to wonder if it was the gap in my front teeth. We're not talking about the Grand Canyon or anything. People with worse teeth formed happy relationships. But by the time I met Eric on that fateful day, I had taken to staring at myself in the mirror, wondering how would I look with a shaved head. Style was my problem. It's okay to be ordinary, so long as you have style. Unfortunately, I did not.

I liked to wear jeans and a T-shirt with the sleeves ripped out. On some people it's a hot look. On me, not so much. My arms are too long for my height, which is five foot eight. In a tank top, I look like an insect. Then there's my hair. Light nondescript brown. Dead straight, with a tuft that won't sit flat where I injured my head as a kid. Hairdressers obsess over that tuft. To them it's as scary as a drive-by shooting or last year's shoes.

There was a time when I tried to dye my troubles away. Being platinum blonde made my pond green eyes seem less muddy and certainly helped me get past bouncers and attract women. I got to dance with babes who normally looked right through me. But sooner or later the music stops and you have to converse or make out. Both take a certain amount of panache. Therein lies another of my problems.

Some people are sexy. It's like they have a *Yes!* beacon beaming from their forehead. I am not one of those people. I think my beacon says *Inhibited*. Back then, it would have been *Desperate*. I had enough problems making successful foreplay conversation, let alone capitalizing on the rare occasions when I made first base with a hottie. To make matters worse, my seduction technique malfunctioned completely over the most trivial things. For example, I would lose focus over crappy tattoos, bulimia, meth labs in the kitchen, and a blithe ignorance of major news matters but an in-depth knowledge of reality television.

If I ever managed to keep a girlfriend for more than a month, it was because she had decided to put up with me and I went along with her decision out of gratitude and hormones. I think we can all agree that in the absence of the ideal woman, having sex with *someone* is better than masturbating alone in your cold bed.

After that disillusioning evening in the bar with Eric, I bought a book called *101 Ways To Improve Your Social Life*. "Become a good listener," it said. "Ask questions that begin 'What do you think of...'" There was a whole chapter devoted to first dates.

I was comforted to know that I was not alone; it was clear from the first few pages that there were other losers out there. But by Chapter Three I realized my problem was much worse than one of limited social repartee. I was a prisoner of romantic delusion. I was marking time, waiting for that special someone to come along, just as Aunt Shirley had predicted. I could imagine my drab life transformed by passion and purpose, myself snugly adrift in coupledom. The trouble was, intelligent fascinating women were not exactly lining up to rescue dull little nobodies like me. If I wanted a tomorrow that included a real relationship, I would have to improve myself.

My first step was to get rid of my television.

Suzie was shocked. "But you almost had a breakdown when *Queer As Folk* ended. How will you live without *The L Word*? Oh, my God...what about *The Daily Show*?"

"If I spend any more time staring at the box, green slime will grow on my teeth," I declared. "It's now or never. I have to get a life."

Suzie gave me a strange look. "It's up to you, but I think you're taking this too far." I knew she wanted to say more, but she held back.

"You're probably right, but the fact is, whatever I've been doing, it's not working. I have to do something different before it's too late. Do you understand?"

"Babe, you're only twenty-six."

"I'll be twenty-seven in a few weeks. There are women my age with four kids."

"Yeah, and look at them." Suzie paused over this scary thought. "Oh fuck, are you telling me you want to have babies or something?"

"Get real. All I'm saying is most people are settling down by now. I feel like a freak."

Suzie stabbed her chest with a finger. "*I* haven't settled down."

"That's because you prefer fucking around."

She didn't deny it. Instead she adopted her most sensible voice. "They say you can try too hard. Just relax and get on with your life. Sooner or later the right woman will come along."

"I don't buy that." I'd given this plenty of thought and had made up my mind. "I don't believe passive wins the day. I'm sick of school. I'm sick of the bookstore. It's time I got serious."

"What are you going to do—go to Europe or something?"

"No. I'm going to change myself and meet new people." I carried my TV to her car. We were taking it down the road to the Community Thrift Store on Valencia.

"But there's nothing wrong with you just the way you are," Suzie said.

I ran a quick mental count of the girlfriends who'd dumped me in the past several years. "Fifteen women can't be wrong."

"Oh, please. Like anyone dates for more than three months at our age."

"Almost everyone we know is in a long-term relationship," I reminded her.

"Whatever."

Suzie bitched about this herself—the diminishing supply of attractive, available women. Suddenly, all the best ones were wearing someone's ring and talking about bathroom renovations instead of their favorite band. I knew our mutual friends wondered why Suzie and I didn't hook up, and maybe I was an idiot for wanting to keep our friendship the way it was. Suzie was all things lovely, from her short dyed copper hair that she wore in two little pigtails on top of her head, to her sparkling blue eyes, which she made ocean bright with cerulean contacts, to her milky skin and tight skirts and the little fluffy sweaters she wore most of the year 'round.

She was shorter than me and worked out so she wouldn't look like a waif. On top of her fetching appearance, she was loyal, funny, and a woman of the world, even though she was only a year older than me. I could have picked worse girlfriends by far, and generally did.

"You still coming over on the weekend?" she asked.

"Sure." One of our married-to-the-woman-of-her-dreams pals from college was having a baby shower. While we were wasted one evening, we'd rashly offered to do the catering.

Suzie closed the hatch on my TV, and as I waved good-bye to living vicariously through lame plot lines and ludicrously thin actresses, she got into the car and hung her head out the window. "Don't do anything rash," she said, as if I would know how.

I smiled and waved good-bye but didn't answer. I needed to do something rash; I was falling asleep at the wheel of my life.

❖

I remember the afternoon we cooked for that baby shower as if it was yesterday. Suzie shared half a Victorian with two other women. We were in the courtyard drinking iced tea after we got done making artichoke dip, falafel, and vegetarian mini-pizzas. Suzie's roommates, Ashleigh and Karla, were trying to repair Karla's favorite vibrator, which had ended up in someone's Jacuzzi. I didn't ask.

Karla said, "Are you really quitting your job, Chance?"

"I wrote my resignation this morning."

Suzie looked horrified.

"Don't worry. I found something else." I fished in my pockets for my new business cards. The design was pink and cut in a poodle silhouette. I handed some around.

"'Canine Follies,'" Suzie read aloud, mortification frozen on her face. "'Dog Grooming With Attitude. Your Canine Care Consultant is Chantelle Delaney.'"

"*Chantelle?*" Karla and Ashleigh echoed.

"Mrs. Van Wynterhaven—that's my new boss—says my full name sounds classier. She doesn't like Chance."

"You don't know the first thing about dogs," Suzie pointed out.

"They're going to train me. That's part of the deal. I go out with another groomer and assist. Then I work for a month under supervision and..." I became conscious of my companions exchanging those nervous, darting looks that happen when no one wants to say what has to be said.

Suzie touched my hand in one of her big-sister gestures. "Have you talked to Dr. Birnbaum?"

"Hell, no." What had I achieved in two years of therapy? Complete inertia, that's what. "I'm in control here. I don't need my therapist's permission to get a new job."

"Dog grooming…" Karla twiddled with the vibrator and it burst abruptly into life. Over the mechanical hum, she continued, "Aren't you kind of overqualified?"

Karla's people were from Connecticut. She tried not to be a snob but it was in her DNA.

I said breezily, "As far as Mrs. Van Wynterhaven is concerned, an MA is a liability. She says college educated people have forgotten how to do an honest day's work."

Karla, who took her own permanent student status seriously, said, "Only someone who hasn't had to write a PhD thesis could say something so ridiculous. Sounds like envy to me."

"Whatever." I had a feeling Kristina Van Wynterhaven had never suffered a moment's pang over missing out on sorority gossip and B-grade lectures while she traveled the world as a personal assistant and dog groomer for the über-rich.

A picture of a foreign princess wearing a tiara, her hand resting on the head of a disdainful dog, hung in the foyer of the Canine Follies office. Underneath it, a caption read something like: *My personal friend and patron, a benefactor of animal welfare charities, H.R.H. Crown Princess Sofia of Castille, photographed with her beloved Borzoi, Grand-Ch. Valshebnik Baron Draco, "Drak."*

Mrs. Van Wynterhaven had worked for this woman years ago in St. Tropez and still received birthday and Christmas gifts from her. She displayed these in a mock Louis XIV cabinet in her office.

"I think poodle grooming is a fine idea," Ashleigh pronounced, serenely Southern. "And a good business too, I'm sure."

I thanked her and gave Suzie a pointed look. I had expected more support from my best friend.

"I know some people with dogs," she managed weakly.

I gave her a bunch of my poodle-shaped cards. "Tell them we do all breeds."

"Hey, Chance. Are you still seeing that dolphin trainer?" Karla asked. "Yvette…was that her name?"

"No, it's Evelyn," I said. "We broke up ages ago."

"You wouldn't have her number, would you? We're trying to fix my cousin up with someone bi."

This perked Suzie up. "Oh my God. Are you talking about the cousin with the Harley and the pierced tongue? Is she queer? I had no idea."

"Calm down," Karla said. "We're talking about the CPA with the bi wife. They're looking for an extra."

"She plays and he watches?" Suzie grimaced. "That's disappointing."

"Sounds like something Evelyn might be into," I muttered. She'd always kept a covert eye on the TV and picked up her cell phone while we were fucking. In the end it got me down and I dumped her before she had time to dump me.

"Can you think of anyone else?" Karla banged the vibrator lightly against her calf. It had died again.

I hadn't dated any other bisexuals, at least not that I knew of. Which meant anything was possible, since I had no idea what went on in the heads of my girlfriends. "If I think of anyone, I'll let you know," I said and stood up. "I need to get going."

Suzie walked me out as far as the gate. "Be careful," she advised, fixing the black velvet ties in her radiant pigtails. "Don't look them in the eye. They think it's aggression."

"Don't worry," I said with a nonchalance I was far from feeling. "They're mostly show dogs."

"Genetically speaking, they're wolves in poodle's clothing."

"Sounds like one of my mom's universal truths."

Suzie giggled. "Sounds like most of my exes."

"We should start a club for women who can't do commitment," I remarked.

Suzie studied me gravely. "I don't think that's us. I mean, you and I have been best friends for ten years. What's that if it isn't commitment?"

She had a point. We weren't incapable, we were just unlucky. I slipped my arm around her waist. "Maybe that's the problem. Maybe other women can't compete."

"You know what?" Suzie said, "That's too fucking bad." And we kissed and hugged like we always did, our love uncomplicated by sex.

CHAPTER TWO

Some dogs relish grooming. Fritz the poodle did not. "You should have been a Mexican hairless dog," I told him as I plucked the hair from inside his ears. "Or maybe a Dalmatian."

I released him and he leapt off the grooming table and fetched his leash.

"Sorry, pal," I said. "This is a grooming visit only."

Fritz sat to perfect attention and stared at me. It's a tough look to resist—hope mingled with adoration. It was the kind of expression I longed to see on a woman's face. After six months on the dog circuit, I was finally becoming hardened. I hung the leash over its hook, ignoring the yelps of dismay.

"Next time," I promised him, heart of stone.

Later that morning I cajoled my van into the steep heart of Pacific Heights, a premium area for grooming—white mansions, the pitter patter of Maltese toenails on parquet floors. My client was Mrs. Goldman, a widow who lived alone. I pressed the buzzer at the side door and the maid answered. She was not the weary apron-and-cap Hispanic woman typically encountered in this neighborhood. Her name was Peaches and she had pink spiky hair and piercings and played in a girl band. Mrs. Goldman, whose son owned a record label, let the band practice in her basement. In exchange, they took turnabout playing maid on the regular staff's day off.

"The old lady's asleep and those fucking animals nearly took my foot off when I tried to clean her bathroom," Peaches informed me, chewing gum at double time.

"They respond to discipline," I said as we trudged upstairs.

Peaches blew a bubble. "Who doesn't? Coffee?"

I shook my head. "Nope. I'll get started. Tight schedule today."

Mrs. Goldman had an area of her enormous bedroom furnished specially for her precious ones. There were dog baths, a grooming table, two tiny four-poster beds, copious toys, and a treadmill. Hendrix and Quatro were gifts from her son, who lived in Beverly Hills and visited once a week to take her to temple. Fragrant little white dogs with satin bows, they were thrilled to see me.

Mrs. Goldman awoke as they yapped. "Are you the hairdresser?" she asked like she'd never seen me before. This was normal.

"No, ma'am. I'm the dog groomer."

"Well, don't just stand there." She propped herself on an elbow. "Get my robe."

The dogs were hysterical. I stuck my head out the door, fruitlessly looking for Peaches, who was better than I was at the personal care stuff but seemed to vanish the moment I arrived. Clearly, my magnetic personality escaped *her* notice as well.

Mrs. Goldman said, "Shush my darlings."

I gave up waiting for Peaches and helped her into her robe.

"It's my kidneys," she said. "Hurry."

We inched our way across an ocean of ivory carpet, Mrs. Goldman clutching my arm in a death grip. The old lady had a touch of Alzheimer's and was soon to have her hips replaced, but first she had to lose eighty pounds.

"You've probably heard of my son, Samuel Goldman," she puffed. "He's in the pop music business."

I nodded and wiggled my fingers, trying to keep the circulation flowing in my arm. We'd had this conversation before.

"I suppose you're a singer. Most of the girls who work here are singers."

"Not me. I have a terrible voice."

"That doesn't stop anyone these days. And the music—if you can call it that. What happened to a good tune? It's all computers now. That's what my son says. You hear about that Milly Vanilla person? She couldn't sing a note."

When we reached the bathroom door I said, "I'll send Peaches up to help you get back in bed."

"Peaches?" Mrs. Goldman looked puzzled.

One of the Maltese chewed on my ankle like my new Docs were rawhide.

"The singer," I reminded her, prying the little beast off.

Mrs. Goldman caught on. "Virgin Blessing. That's her band. My son says they have a future."

I imagined Peaches and her buddies snorting coke in a stretch limo after gracelessly accepting a Grammy. "No kidding?"

Mrs. Goldman leaned against her bathroom door frame and wheezed, "What's your name, girl?"

"Chance."

She peered at me for a moment. "Well, Chance, this is your lucky day. See that?" She pointed a chubby bejeweled finger at the computer workstation at the far end of her bedroom. "It's yours."

"No, Mrs. Goldman. That's your computer, the one your son gave you so you can do e-mail."

"They're not getting my credit card number." She glowered. "If you don't take it out of here, it's going in the trash."

I vacillated. What if Mrs. Goldman forgot she'd given it to me and thought she had been robbed? What would her son say when he found out?

"Do you want it or not? Don't they teach young people manners anymore?"

"I'll take it," I said. "Thank you, Mrs. Goldman. I'll take it away with me when I'm done, okay?"

"Fine," she said. "Now come here and help me with these toenails."

❖

After scoring costly technology and a tip for the unplanned human pedicure, I had an appointment with Dr. Death, a Doberman who had tried to eat her last groomer. The dog wasn't to blame, said my boss. She'd had pups and the owner had failed to inform Canine Follies.

The usual groomer was on holiday. The replacement had needed ten stitches. We were well insured against such eventualities and even had "death and dismemberment" coverage. Nice.

Dr. Death was owned by yuppies who had a house just off Lombard in the Marina District. The place was plastered in warning stickers that depicted a drooling dog with teeth like Jaws. The small print said, "The owners accept no liability for injury or death sustained by persons illegally on these premises. You have been warned."

Wearing padded leather gloves and a flak jacket, I inserted a passkey in the front door. Dr. Death was on the other side baying for blood. Wedging the door with my foot, I opened it a crack and tossed in a piece of steak and an old T-shirt of mine. Dr. Death munched, then inspected the T-shirt and wagged her tail, apparently remembering the priceless moments we'd shared.

It was time to be assertive. I said, "Sit," and she responded instantly, her nose working overtime. "Yes, I've been with others," I admitted, extending a leather mitt.

She took my hand gently in her teeth and led me to the living room. Her great passion was to watch *The Sound of Music* on DVD while I groomed her. She particularly relished the raindrops on roses song. I particularly relished Julie Andrews emerging dripping wet from the lake.

The yuppies were expecting their first baby and unlike Dr. Death, Mrs. Yuppie would not wake up one morning to find her offspring had been sold to strangers. I supposed dog owners needed to convince themselves their pets would soon forget just as people insisted unwed teenage mothers would "get over" giving their babies up for adoption.

As I soaped Dr. Death, I wondered about my own mother. Had she felt there was no choice? Had her life been made a living hell? The scenario I most often imagined involved a bright young coed whose boyfriend claims the baby is not his and whose parents threaten to throw her out unless she gives the child up. I could see my birth mother holding me for a few precious moments, shedding tears on my tiny scrunched face. Then a stern nurse with a compressed bosom tears me from her arms and banishes me to some far-flung nursery to lie sobbing with all the other lonely babies waiting for an approved couple.

It heartened me to picture the joy of my adoptive parents the first time they held me in their arms. Mom often told me that story. After seven miscarriages and ten years of dashed hopes, they had thought they would never have the little baby they longed for. Then one day there was a phone call from the lawyer and Mom was so excited she drove over the speed limit all the way to Dad's office to tell him in person. They did a two-step around the coffee machine with Dad's secretary sobbing to see them so happy.

There was photographic evidence of their love and devotion. An entire album for each year of my childhood, even after the divorce. Their love made me ashamed to think about my birth mother at all. Yet there was an empty place where her face needed to be. I must have seen her when I was born. Some sleepless nights I tried to connect to that ancient memory, concentrating on my dark ceiling until it dissolved into a set of blurred features and I was almost certain she was smiling at me.

The nuns were singing about solving a problem like Maria and Dr. Death was baying right along with them. I trimmed her toenails and buffed them with an emery board. To my surprise, I heard the front door open and Dr. Death bounded off, returning a moment later with a white-faced Mrs. Yuppie.

"Hey there." She gingerly sat down. "Chantelle, isn't it?"

I nodded. "Can I get you a glass of water, ma'am? You look awful."

She moaned and held on to her stomach. "Morning sickness."

I got the water and steadied her hand on the glass as she sipped. She was ice cold and trembling, and the dog first aid course had not covered owners. "Want me to call your doctor?" I asked, terrified that she was going to go into labor or something.

She shook her head. "It's okay. This is normal."

"I think you better lie down." I helped her to her feet. She swayed. I put my arm around her. "Where's your room?"

"I'm going to be sick," she said, dry retching.

I half dragged her into the nearest bathroom and looked the other way while she threw up. Afterward she sank down onto the cold tiles and started to cry.

Wanting to escape before things got any worse, I said, "I'll phone your husband."

"No," she cried. "Please. He never wanted this. It was me. I wanted it." She wept some more.

I wanted to say: *It's his baby too. Maybe he would be horrified to think of his wife crawling across the bathroom floor.* But it was none of my business. I helped her to her feet and half carried her to the bedroom.

"Please, could you get me some Gatorade? It's in the fridge." She took some pills from her bedside drawer.

I fetched the Gatorade and sat with her for a few minutes, feeling angry that it was me and not the husband who was caring for her, angry at her martyred insistence on going through this alone. Was that how she would cope with their baby too? After she'd stopped gagging, I left the room and found the husband's work phone number in my organizer. I got his secretary. He was in a meeting, she said, and could not be disturbed.

I said, "Tell him it's the dog groomer. Tell him I only got as far as the toenails because I spent the whole appointment looking after his wife. Tell him I'm worried about leaving her lying half conscious in bed, and he needs to come home *right now*. Do you understand me?"

"Calm down," said the secretary. "Are you saying the dog is sick?"

I counted to three then, in my most patient tone, said, "Listen very carefully. Your boss's pregnant wife is sick."

Brief silence. The phone clicked. A man said, "Catherine? Honey?"

I explained who I was and what was going on.

He said "Oh God" several times and, "Why didn't she tell me?" and, "Well, she's not shutting me out of this too."

He asked me to wait at the apartment until he got there. I said sure. It was only my lunch hour. When he arrived, he stuffed a hundred bucks into my hand and virtually ran to the bedroom. I packed my grooming case, made change, and wrote a note saying I'd be back to finish Dr. Death in three days time.

Mr. Yuppie emerged as I was heading to the door. He insisted I keep the change as a tip. "I suppose she told you I don't want this baby," he said, mistaking me for Dr. Phil. "Well, that was before she got pregnant. Okay?" He opened the door for me. "I want this baby. If anything like this ever happens again while you're here, please call the doctor right away."

"Sure. No problem." I eased my way past him, hoping there was nothing else he needed to share.

"Thanks for calling me," he added. "You did the right thing."

No shit? I stuffed the extra sixty bucks in my pocket and said, "I hope Mrs. Pederson feels better soon, sir."

CHAPTER THREE

Sensible, fun-loving lesbian, 26, seeks similar. Let's get together and see what happens.

"That's it?" Suzie looked up with a pained expression.

"I hate those self-indulgent ads about walking in the rain and living for the moment," I said. "It's not like you can get to know someone from a paragraph printed in the personals. People can make up any bullshit."

"And they do," Eric said.

"I'll get replies," I said.

Suzie grunted. "Yeah, from geeks."

Eric gave me a quizzical stare. "Is that really what you're looking for—sensible and fun-loving...twenty-six? You want to...*see what happens?*"

"It's a start."

"Babe, you never date women your own age," Suzie said. "There's no chemistry."

I marveled at this insight. Suzie was right. The only women I'd ever been hot for were older than me.

"Let's rewrite this shall we, sweetie?" Eric picked up a pen.

Romantic lesbian, 26, seeks charming woman in her thirties who likes sex and wants a serious relationship.

Suzie gave her endorsement. "Tasteful, but covers the important bases."

"Take out the sex bit," I said.

Eric raised his eyebrows. "You want a platonic relationship?"

"Of course not, but—"

"Eric's right," Suzie said. "Lesbians leave out the sex bit far too often."

"Unlike gay men," I was stung to respond. "I mean, imagine if we ran ads like this." I scribbled an example.

Horny dyke can't get enough pussy. If you've got big tits let's fuck.

"Now that would get replies," Eric said.

"Yes, but from whom?"

Suzie was laughing into her beer. "Probably from me."

"You're not that desperate," I said.

"I am. Trust me."

Suzie always had a date, so this seemed unlikely. But it was sweet of her to try to make me feel better.

Eric said, "*Bound* is playing at the Castro again. Want to go?"

I hesitated. I love movies. But I'd seen *Bound* at least fifty times.

Suzie gave Eric a nudge. "I thought you had a hot date for tonight."

"I did until he had his cat declawed."

I said, "You're kidding." When would our veterinary surgeons refuse to practice this barbarism like they did in most civilized countries? I felt ashamed.

"It's a requirement in some apartments," Suzie informed us. "Maybe he had no choice."

Eric shook his head. "Ryan didn't want his new furniture scratched. It got me thinking about what people will sink to for the sake of appearances."

Now that he was back in town, he had a yen to settle down, Eric explained wistfully. All he wanted was a fascinating lover who knew how to cook; someone stylish, hot, and intellectual from a compatible star sign. He had been dating Ryan for several optimistic months. Now this.

"So, you've dumped him?" Suzie asked.

"Not in so many words. I told him I needed time."

Guilty about leaping to judgment, I groped for an excuse that would enable my friend to give this promising relationship a chance. "Maybe the cat was savage."

"Oh, please." Eric rolled his eyes. "C'mon. I don't feel like seeing the damned movie anyway. Let's take a walk."

For reasons of nostalgia, he drove us down to Fisherman's Wharf, where we shoved our way through knots of tourists exchanging Alcatraz stories as they lined up for overpriced seafood. Out on the pier, the breeze was fresh and salty. We leaned on the rail, staring at the lights shimmering on the water.

"My dad used to bring us here every summer," Eric said. "We'd stay at the Holiday Inn and take day trips to Sausalito."

"Where are you from originally?" I asked.

"San Diego. But I moved here as soon as I graduated high school. The past few years I've been in England. My ex is an Oxford don."

"Do your parents know about you?"

"Yeah. But I haven't really been on speaking terms with Dad since I came out."

Was this a huge loss? "You used to get along okay?"

Pensively, Eric said, "I thought so. We have things in common. The old man's an opera nut. We used to play golf together."

Suzie buttoned her purple monster jacket over her yellow fluffy sweater. Shoving her hands deep in the pockets, she said, "Sometimes I wish my parents would disown me. But no. Every Sunday the phone call. 'Did you go to church? Why don't you write? Even your cousin Eileen writes. Have you met a nice boy yet?'"

Suzie's folks lived in a small town somewhere in the Midwest. She was one of seven children. Four of them were gay, but Mom and Dad just pretended it wasn't happening. I had met them a few years back. All they could talk about was Suzie's oldest brother, who was a partner in a funeral home, and how he'd just embalmed a guy who weighed over five hundred pounds.

"Dad's sick," Eric said after Suzie lapsed into silence. "I'm going down to visit him again soon."

I stared up at the stars and tried to remember where scientists said you can see 51-Pegasi, the planet that proved there were other solar systems just like ours and intelligent life might exist in some other galaxy. I couldn't even find the constellation of Pegasus, much less a tiny pinpoint off to one side.

"Do you think he'll talk to you this time?" Suzie asked.

"He's in a coma. So he'll have to listen for once."

"They say unconscious people can still hear," I said, wanting to offer some small consolation since Eric seemed upset.

"I suppose it's selfish, in a way." He frowned. "I'm frightened he'll go and I'll never get to say some things I need to say to him. So it's about me, really."

"And that's okay, sweetie." Suzie grabbed him and hugged him hard. "God, there's so much unresolved stuff between you and your dad."

As we walked back to Eric's custom yellow Packard, I thought about how lucky I was. As soon as I'd realized I was a lesbian, I gave my mother a copy of *Patience and Sarah* and a photo of me wearing a tux. She was quiet at first, then she asked me to bring my girlfriends home to meet her. Now both my parents are card-carrying members of PFLAG and turn out to march for Gay Pride with a banner that says *Our Children Deserve Our Unconditional Love*, as if bigots will suddenly have an epiphany when they read that important sentiment. Still, I was proud of them. My parents might be flakes but they weren't hypocrites.

Lately they were at me to settle down. Mom had been thinking about the commitment ceremony and had asked her guru if he would officiate. Last time I visited, she gave me a photocopy of a magazine article on donor insemination. I felt like a total failure admitting I had no immediate prospects.

Eric drove us around for a while and we ended up on Folsom. He saw a guy he knew outside the Hole in the Wall Saloon and sounded the horn. A man in a studded harness waved a gloved paw in salute.

"Have you been in there?" I asked, impressed and horrified all at once.

"Sure," Eric said. "Want to go see?"

"Maybe some other time."

Suzie laughed. "Chance has led a sheltered life."

"I'm not naïve," I objected. "I had a girlfriend who tied me up."

"She tied you up once," Suzie said. "And, if I recall correctly, you broke your bed trying to get loose and she dumped you."

"I would have dumped her anyway."

It wasn't being tied up that had bothered me. It was the fact that I almost dislocated a shoulder when I had an orgasm and she was so trashed she couldn't get the knots undone and they got tighter instead. Eventually she fetched my neighbor, a gay fashion victim who couldn't stop snickering while he cut me free. We should never have used rope, he lectured. The sexually sophisticated chose leather or canvas. And they learned how to tie knots.

We changed direction and cruised along Market past the grubby pavements and bag ladies. As we passed the Church Street Station and headed into the homosphere, I glanced up at The Cafe remembering the good old days when it was more lesbian and Suzie and I would hang out on the patio after school. We turned onto Castro and wound down our windows to tap into the cheerful micro-climate. I felt a pang as we passed the bookstore. I had been safe and happy there for two years, as cloistered from the real world as a Carmelite nun.

"Want to hang out somewhere?" Eric asked.

Suzie shook her head. "I'm tired."

"Then I'll take you right on home, ma'am. How 'bout you, Miss Chance?"

"I've still got to write that personal ad."

"We could write it together over a nightcap," Eric offered.

I hesitated, but it occurred to me that he wanted company. He'd been moody lately. "Sure. If you've got nothing else to do."

Eric stopped outside Suzie's place on 18th Street, and she kissed his cheek and got out, leaving the passenger door open so I could switch to the front seat. We waited while she let herself indoors, then Eric said, "Let's go organize that hot date for you."

An hour later we were in my tiny living room composing scintillating personal ad copy for the *Bay Times*. My apartment in the Mission was the smallest of three in a converted Victorian house a few blocks from Suzie's place, just before Valencia. I lived alone. I could afford to because my parents insisted on paying half the rent until I settled down and bought a townhouse with Ms. Right, who would hopefully be a shrink or one of those conventional doctors who also believed in natural therapies.

Sitting at my table, Eric was surrounded by electrical cables and computer manuals. As per usual, he was too gorgeous to live, but I had almost gotten past the point of looking at him and feeling cheated. I had accepted him for what he was—a hair shirt, unsettling proof that human sexuality was complicated. If I could be fooled into finding a man attractive, what did that say about me?

Suzie had told me not to think about it too much or my head would explode. She held up Johnny Depp as an example. Here was a man who made people of all persuasions break a sweat. Imagine being a straight guy sitting next to his girlfriend during *Finding Neverland,* realizing *he* also had a stupid look on his face during the close-ups of Johnny.

Eric assembled Mrs. Goldman's computer in less time than it took me to make a bunch of brownies. We'd smoked some weed and now needed sugar. "It's all set up for the Net," he said. "Same ISP as mine. Want to take a look? We can use my dialup. I have broadband now, but I keep AOL in case anything goes wrong."

I shrugged. "Sure." I had a vague idea what he was talking about. I had used the Internet, of course. We had e-mail at the store. And a Web site. But I had never done more than the usual searches. My laptop had died not long after I finished college and hadn't bothered to replace it. I didn't live online like some people.

Eric tapped away on the keyboard, then turned to me with a wayward grin and said, "You haven't seen personals till you've seen this. Let's swing by gay.com and see what's happening."

"Gay.com?"

"Chat. Cyber is one big singles bar, babe. This place is really more for guys, but you'll get the idea." I watched over his shoulder as a hip-looking black and charcoal screen appeared, tastefully arrayed with pictures of pretty boys and muscle Marys. "Now what shall we call you?"

"Me?"

"You're the one with the working parts. We have to give you a profile before you can chat. Think up a name for your log-in."

"What's wrong with Chance?"

Eric shrugged. "Most people don't use their own names. The thing about chat is it's anonymous. I usually go for something philosophical."

My mom's middle name seemed as good as any, so I said, "Make it Faith."

"And the profile?"

"Do I have to?"

"No. But you're looking for a response, so let's do this...." He entered "cute and sane in SF," then got up and ordered me to take his place. Once I'd filled in the rest of the details, he said, "Now click on 'Enter Chat' and we'll see if we can get someone to take the bait."

I stared at the black type on the plain white screen. Eric was scrolling down a list of rooms called things like BBW and Russian Queer Women. "Here's where it shows you who's in each room," he explained, indicating a list of occupants. "Then you can click on a name and see the person's profile. Choose one."

I pointed at random and he clicked on "Geri." A profile appeared at the bottom of the screen. It said "Geri: horny bicurious / blonde 120 shaved / older women pvt me and I'll be ur kinky slut."

"Oh, my God." I reached for the mouse and clicked on the next name.

"They're not all bisexuals or guys pretending to be lesbians," Eric said. "But if I were you, I'd Google for some women-only chats. Once you get to know a few people online you can check to see if they're in a room, then you can go in and talk to them. If you like someone, you can add her to your contacts on Messenger and IM each other any time you want."

I suppose most addictions are born of curiosity. After Eric had gone, I tracked down a few other lesbian chat rooms and watched line after line scroll by. Sometimes I responded to questions. *Where are you from? How old are you?* Mostly, I watched the experts. Women flirted and vanished into private chats. The talk was occasionally fun and witty, but mostly really dumb, even worse than the drivel you have to endure trying to pick up women in bars. It was harmless and meaningless, and banal beyond belief. I was totally hooked.

When someone called Foxy asked me if I wanted to chat in private, I said, "Why not?" and, in an instant, I found myself alone in a box on a screen with a person I had never seen, whose real name I didn't know, and who promptly explained that she was ready to lick me anywhere.

I laughed so hard I almost choked. Somewhere in the back of my mind a small voice ordered me to click the X button and turn off the computer. But instead I told Foxy that I was feeling hot. Then, while she described licking my labia, I went out to the kitchen and made myself a turkey sandwich. I felt strangely elated. I could almost hear the mermaids singing.

CHAPTER FOUR

Her profile said "Reverie: tempting the Fates." We had spoken a few times in an Intellectuals and Artists chat room I frequented because I didn't want to become a regular in Singles Seeking. That seemed tragically uncool. Reverie was from CA. 30. Smart. Polite. Witty. Sensitive. At least that's how it read.

<Reverie> I missed you on the weekend. Were you away?
> I had to work. I missed you too.
<Reverie> Would you care to talk in private, Faith?
> Sure.

A new window opened with her name and mine printed along the top. I closed out the other screens, then keyed in, "Hey." I felt odd being alone with her. Was she really a woman? Did she want cybersex?

She answered my unspoken thought. "I was hoping we could have an actual conversation. Interested?"

I said, "Sure. What do you want to talk about?" I dredged the dim recesses of my mind for a topic I knew well enough to impress her. She did not seem the type who would get excited by dog-grooming horror stories.

"Let's talk about sex," she said.

A lurch of disappointment cramped my gut and for one queasy moment I anticipated the demise of our tantalizing connection with some shriveling line like *Are you wearing panties?* or *Wanna cum, baby?*

"I was thinking about it just the other day." Her words popped onto my screen. "How sex can inspire acts of madness. People destroy lives. Wars are fought. And for what?"

I said, "You're asking the wrong person."

"You don't have sex?"

"Sometimes. But I'm no expert."

"Does the topic bother you? We can change it."

I hesitated. "Well, it's not something people talk about, is it? I mean frankly and honestly."

"You noticed?" There was a smile between the lines.

"I know they talk about it all the time in chat rooms," I said. "But it's…"

"The fast food approach," she supplied. "Yes…it's an odd dichotomy. I mean, how people can be so prudish in a culture so obsessed with sex."

"Yep. It's ironic," I agreed.

"Tell me, do you cyber?" she asked.

I thought about Foxy and several experiments just like her, one of which was obviously a man who'd gotten his ideas from those porn flicks where supposed lesbians are making out in white stiletto heels and long fingernails…as we do. "Technically, I have."

"Technically?"

"I was curious. It was strictly casual."

"Oh? I suppose you're going to tell me it didn't mean anything, huh?" She added, "LMAO," which is Internet-speak for "laughing my ass off."

I cracked up. "To be honest, I found it pretty boring. Call me crazy, but I have this thing for skin."

"Oh, you're one of those throwbacks who actually wants to smell her lover?"

"Shh," I begged. "The cyberpolice might hear you. How about you? Do you do it?"

"I used to. Years ago when chat was a big novelty, before phone sex took off. But I'd feel strange about it now. I've met too many chat widows."

"Women whose lovers have left them for someone they met online?"

"Yes. I was talking to this woman whose partner moved out after fourteen years together. She'd only met the other woman once in real life. Go figure."

"You don't believe people can fall in love in cyberspace?" I'd been thinking about that lately.

The screen was blank for a moment. Then her words slowly appeared. "I think it's possible to mistake an interactive fantasy for love."

"Isn't it that way in real life too? I mean, isn't fantasy the bedrock of romance?"

"Yes, but in real life it's harder to delude yourself because you're working in more than one dimension. I mean, for a start you know what your partner looks like."

"I'm 120 lbs, blonde, 36C 24 34," I lied.

She said, "Uh-huh."

"Okay. Make that Quasimodo and a chocolate addict. How about you?"

"I'm ordinary. You'd never notice me in a crowd."

I smiled to myself at the evasive reply. She was beautiful. I could tell. I forgot to type my next line.

She filled the blank. "Why do you come here?"

I thought for a moment. The bottom line was I was looking for a lover. But I wanted to seem more interesting than that, so I answered, "I like the way fate throws people together. You get to meet women you would never encounter in real life."

"Like us."

"Yes. It's a kaleidoscope in a way," I mused. "It seems completely random, yet there's a pattern. How about you? Why do you come here?"

"It feels safe." A pause. "God. What does that say about me!"

I understood exactly what she meant. I didn't want to examine my online habit too closely either. I tried to imagine her voice. Was it soft and smooth or a husky drawl?

"I suppose everyone here is lonely on some level," she said. "It's the human condition and this place is just a microcosm."

"We have this incredible technology and what do we use it for? Getting a date."

"Intimacy is a casualty of our times," she said. "Is it any wonder people try to compensate."

"Do you think our rapport is a mirage?" I asked, groping for a way to explain that I felt connected to her somehow, that she was more than words on a screen.

"It's a mirage we share." She added <smile>.

I hesitated, then typed, "Would you stop talking to me if I sent you a photo and I didn't look the way you expected?"

She was slow to respond. I read the question over and over and wondered if she had gone. Maybe an incoming Yahoo message had garnered her attention. Maybe she was chatting to someone else in another room at the very same time as she was talking to me. I wondered if I should just click on the X and close our chat down.

Finally her response popped up. "I am silver and exact. I have no preconceptions."

I recognized the line from a semester of poetry. "Sylvia Plath?"

"Yes! You're into poetry?"

"Not really. Just a lucky guess."

"I don't believe in luck," she said. "I believe in Fate."

"And I believe we just changed the subject."

<smile>, she responded.

"We should do this more often," I said.

"What? Talk about sex?"

"Talk in private. I like that no one can interrupt. I get sick of saying hello and good-bye to strangers called Bi-curious Betty all the time."

"Are you asking me to go cyber-steady?"

"Even scarier. I want your Messenger ID." I hoped that sounded more blasé than I felt.

"You're incorrigible," she said, ignoring my request. "Same time Friday?"

I said yes and we exchanged good-byes. I held the room open until the message appeared: *Reverie has left private chat.* I touched her name with my finger, then, feeling silly, I closed the room out and turned off the computer. I could see a mark on the screen where my flesh had connected with the cold glass.

I prowled the kitchen and found some hummus in the fridge. In my mind's eye, a familiar image stirred, a woman with dark hair and indistinct features. I told myself to get real. Reverie probably wasn't the mysterious siren beckoning me from a romantic future. Later, in bed,

I lay awake haunted by her presence. A breeze tugged at my curtains. I closed my eyes, willing sleep to defeat me, but all I could feel was her phantom breath on my cheek, her phantom heart thudding against mine.

❖

"I don't suppose you'd consider marrying me?" Eric dazzled me with his most alluring smile.

"Get serious," I said, scrolling through the replies to my latest online personal ad. There were dozens.

Eric was lying on the faded brocade sofa that for most of my life had occupied a wall in my bedroom. When I moved to the city, I'd bought a queen-size bed, which was never the same after the bondage incident. So I'd replaced it with a new king bed, which meant nothing else would fit into my bedroom. So the sofa was now living room furniture along with my Welsh dresser.

Eric reached for a brownie from the plate I'd deposited on the coffee table earlier. "You can't blame a guy for asking."

"As if." I scanned an e-mail. "Hey, get this one. I'm thirty-two, independent and gentle with a sense of humor, and I cook a great breakfast. If you're tired of meaningless encounters and interested in old-fashioned romance, call me."

"I wish someone would say that to me," Eric muttered.

"Shall I call her?"

"If you don't, I will."

I waded through the next ten e-mails. "All bisexuals," I groaned. "I don't get it. I advertise for a lesbian and thousands of married women reply. Oh great. This one says hubby is built and will join in."

"Three hundred pounds and a hairy back," Eric said.

I choked on my brownie.

"So are you going to call her?" he asked.

I clicked back and read her e-mail again. "Old-fashioned romance." What exactly did that mean? No kissing on the first date?

Eric handed me the phone.

"Not with you sitting there!" I protested.

He gave me a long-suffering look and extracted a cigarette from the antique gold case he kept in his back pocket. "Okay, so I'll go abuse my lungs. In years to come, just keep in mind my emphysema will be on *your* shoulders."

I waited until he had left the room and closed the French doors to my miniscule patio, then I dialed. My fingers felt damp.

A woman answered, "Good evening."

For what seemed an eternity my voice froze in my throat, then I found a stringy croak. "Hello. Is this Hayley?"

"Yes, it is." Her tone was warm and mellow.

I said, "You e-mailed me. My name is Chance."

"Twenty-six and wants an over-thirty who likes sex?"

I blushed. "Um. Well." Where was a good line when you needed it?

"You're shy?" A soft laugh. She sounded like a grown-up.

Through the French doors, Eric made encouraging sign language at me and mimed a drinking gesture.

"We could discuss that over a drink," I said with borrowed suave.

"Sounds good. Do you know Marlena's?"

"The drag place in Hayes Valley?" A somewhat surprising choice, I thought. On the other hand, it meant there would be plenty to look at if we were bored with each other after three minutes. "Sure, I know it. Would Friday suit you?"

"Seven-thirty. I'll be at the bar. Blonde. Pearl earrings."

"I'll be there," I said. "Thank you." I hung up the phone and beamed at Eric.

He stubbed out his cigarette and returned. "Well?"

"Friday night. She's blonde."

"I'll bet she is." With a satisfied air, he helped himself to another brownie.

I glanced past him to my computer and was suddenly flooded with guilt. "Damn. I have a chat date Friday night."

Eric raised an eyebrow. "She'll understand."

"You think so? You think it's okay if I call her back and make a different time?"

Eric froze midway through a bite. "Let me clarify something," he said in a slow, precise manner. "You are thinking of canceling an actual date with a living, breathing woman so you can chat online with someone you've never laid eyes on?"

Framed in those terms it sounded like I'd lost my mind. "Okay, so I can e-mail Reverie." I felt an icy grip close on my heart. "No problem."

"Don't you have her phone number yet?" Eric asked.

I shook my head. I had offered mine but she seemed uncomfortable about swapping so I let it go. "We decided not to do that yet."

"Really?"

For some reason I felt defensive. I'd been hurt when Reverie avoided exchanging phone numbers. I was still trying to fathom why she didn't trust me. I longed to hear her voice and had hoped she felt the same way about me. Evidently not.

"Reverie has had a couple of bad experiences," I said feebly.

"With women she met online? They got together in real time?"

I hesitated. She had been vague about the details. "I think so."

Eric shrugged and picked up his jacket. "Well, you get to kiss a few frogs no matter how you meet people. Have fun on Friday."

I gave him a bleak little smile. I finally had a date. I should have been ecstatic.

CHAPTER FIVE

Marlena's in Hayes Valley used to be a neighborhood bar but was now a watering hole for drag queens. It was a friendly place, even if you weren't wearing lipstick and size twelve pumps. Dim lights bounced off countless mini–disco balls and Star Wars memorabilia plastered the walls. On the tiny stage someone was lip-synching Madonna's version of "Fever."

I thought instantly of Turkmenistan, where they'd just banned this important art form as a scourge on their culture, along with opera and ballet. Eric had asked me to read a letter he wrote to their president recently, protesting these Neanderthal measures, as if a guy who named towns, schools, and meteorites after himself would give a crap about the opinions of others. He had probably lost a karaoke contest or something. A ban on lip-synching. What was his problem?

I stared around, looking for a blonde with pearl earrings. There were at least ten of them. Two who weren't wearing wigs were sitting at the bar in conversation. I wondered if I had stumbled into an interview situation where the candidate before me was still there. Suppressing an urge to leave and rush back home in case Reverie was online, I applauded the queen on the stage and joined in the general excitement when the door opened and a six-foot brunette in a torch-singer gown swept in, followed by a fawning entourage of Trannyshack types.

Someone rushed up to the glittering newcomer, got down on his knees, and begged for the privilege of drinking champagne from her shoe. She allowed him to fondle her thigh, just above a spangled garter. After he was done pawing her, one of the entourage led him away and the bartender rushed to escort her to the best table in the place, which had been reserved. Once she was seated, all kinds of people sidled over to kiss the gloved hand she extended. I was tempted to join them. How often do you see genuine glamour anymore? If this was the only thrill in store for me tonight, I felt okay about missing my chat date.

I had e-mailed Reverie to make another time. Having to do this made me nervous. My excuse was an after-hours appointment. I didn't say anything about meeting someone who had answered a personal ad. But I had a weird feeling she would know. Before I left, I checked my e-mail. No reply. Was she angry? Had she even gotten my e-mail? What if she turned up to wait for me and I didn't show?

To be safe, I sent another e-mail telling her that I hoped she'd gotten the first one. Even as I clicked "send," I knew I was doing something irrational but I could not help myself. The ephemeral nature of our connection rattled me. I feared one day she would vanish and I would be left wondering if some terrible accident had befallen her or if she had merely found another cyberite in another chat room out there in the virtual meat market.

The thought pulled me up short. I was in a real bar in the real world and a real woman was waiting to meet me. What did it matter if someone I had never even seen vanished from my life? Forcing confidence into my stride, I went up to the counter and ordered a scotch because it seemed more sophisticated than beer. It was obvious that everyone in the room knew exactly why I was there. At least that's how it felt. Wanting to hide behind something, I wished I were a smoker. That's what cell phones and iPods were for, I decided. They were cigarette stand-ins.

My wristwatch said 7:36 p.m. Perhaps she was running late. I stole a look at the two blondes whose hair was their own. One of them caught my eye and smiled. A small bead of perspiration trickled between my shoulder blades. I smiled back.

The younger of the pair gazed at me more intently. "Chance?"

"Hayley?"

She shook my hand warmly. "Pleased to meet you." Her companion gave me a polite nod. "This is my sister Viv. I hope we didn't confuse you. Viv was coming home this way so she's been keeping me company until you showed."

I greeted Viv and asked, "Can I get you both a drink?"

Viv shook her head. "No, thanks. I have to get going." She murmured something to her sister, bestowed a half-smile on me, and strolled off.

"There's a table just over there," Hayley said when our drinks were poured. "Shall we?"

I picked up our glasses and accompanied her across the room. She smelled faintly of a light floral scent. It suited her. There was a softness about her, a warmth in her eyes and a gentle manner that put me at ease.

"I like this place," she said, sitting down. "There's always someone fabulous to look at."

I was quick to agree. "Yes, and you can actually have a conversation."

She didn't seem nervous. I suspected she had done this before. I felt like the novice I was.

As if she could read my mind, she said, "Is this your first time?"

"You can tell?"

"I imagine you don't usually place ads. You must find it easy to pick up women."

I nearly said: *Are you insane?* But she seemed serious.

"Well, that's a nice compliment," I responded. "So tell me, how did you slip through the net? Are the folks in your circle slow or something?"

A dimple appeared in her cheek. "My friends say I'm too choosy."

"Is that a euphemism for having high standards?"

"Probably. The older I get, the less patient I am with the games people play." She was suddenly serious. "I want to be with another adult. It doesn't seem that unreasonable, does it?"

"Nope." *An adult.* I was not sure if I would qualify.

She frowned. "I suppose I must sound jaded."

"No, you sound like a realist."

"What can I say? I'm over thirty. Been there done that." She toyed with the olive in her cocktail. "So tell me about yourself, Chance."

I considered my options and went for complete honesty. "I don't want to waste your time, Hayley. I have a feeling I'm probably not what you are looking for. I am quite unsettled right now. Actually, I have no idea what I am doing."

She didn't seem upset by this litany. In fact, her kind eyes were full of sympathy. "Did you break up recently?"

"No. I just changed my job and decided to stop working on my PhD for a while. And I haven't been in a steady relationship for ages."

"Have you ever been in something long term?"

"I was in one of those on-again off-again situations for a couple of years." I cast my mind back to Cecilia. We'd never been able to figure out whether we should be friends or lovers. In the end we were neither. I still regretted that.

"What's your new job?" Hayley asked.

"I groom dogs."

That earned a moment's silence. "Dogs," she repeated.

I waited, intrigued. Reactions to my job told me a great deal about the women I talked with. Some delivered a polite brush-off and looked around for the nearest dentist or banker. Others immediately produced a photograph of their dog for my admiration. One had inquired if I had a collar and leash she could try on.

"Did you have to get vaccinated against rabies?" Hayley asked.

I blinked. "Yes. It was quite a shot."

"I remember. I had one when I went to India. Monkey bites are the main problem over there."

"Wow. India." I wondered instantly if travel was the answer to my quest for a personality transplant. "Do they really let cows wander the streets?"

She laughed. "Sacred cows are big in the north. You're supposed to step aside for them in the markets. I was told off by a *sadhu*—that's a holy man—when I pushed one away after it tried to eat my lunch."

I thought about my parents, who'd recently gotten back after a month in an ashram in Bangalore, studying the knowledge of breath with His Holiness, Sri Sri Ravi Shankar, not to be confused with the musician. I hadn't wanted to go, and I wondered now if that was a mistake. Maybe next time I'd be more open minded when they invited me on one of their spiritual awareness vacations.

"It must be fantastic to see places like that," I said. "Did you go by yourself?"

"No. Viv came along for the ride."

We talked about travel and global warming for a while, bypassed the war and who was rolling in profits because of it, just in case we were on opposite sides of the political divide, then I ordered more drinks.

"You've had some real adventures," I said. "It must be pretty tame being back home working nine to five."

"I'm glad I got a chance to see the world," Hayley said. "But I'm ready to settle down now."

"Have you ever been truly in love?" I asked, then added quickly, "I'm sorry. That's a personal question."

Hayley laughed. "Oh, you should hear some of the things women want to know on blind dates."

I could only imagine. "Is that why you bring your sister along?"

"I don't take any chances when I'm meeting someone for the first time. You should be careful too. Phone a friend at an arranged time or get someone to wait in the car. The Internet is great, but you can't take anything for granted. You always have to be careful about the face-to-face stage."

"I've never thought about it," I confessed, picturing Suzie's face if she knew I had done this without telling her. I'd avoided answering her questions about my progress with the personal ads.

She toyed with her drink. "It's a jungle out there. But I've also met some really nice women. Made some good friends."

I was suddenly overwhelmed with guilt. There was a melancholy in her smile that told me she was weary. At her age it was too soon to give up on the idea of finding a soulmate, but the way she gripped her glass told me she was close. Too much disillusionment could do that for anyone. If a woman as decent and attractive as Hayley could not find Ms. Right, what hope did I have?

She searched my face. "No chemistry for you either, huh?"

I swallowed too much scotch in a gulp of shame mixed with relief. Coughing, I said, "Maybe it's too soon to know."

"I don't think instant attraction is the only barometer, but it's kind of hard to move forward without it." She touched my hand very gently. "I'm glad you came. I hope you find her."

"You too." I got up as she stood. I liked her quiet dignity, the womanly shape of her. I liked the way she tucked her hair behind one ear. I wished there had been magic between us.

We walked in silence to her car. Her sister was in the passenger seat reading the latest Nora Roberts. I opened the door and Hayley gave me a brief hug.

"Don't settle," she said. "Someone always ends up with a broken heart."

❖

Back home, I almost ran to the computer, peeling off my jacket and telling myself I didn't need to use the bathroom immediately. I dialed up, whispering all the while *go fast go fast* and cursing that I didn't have broadband. It took a frustrating forty seconds to load Messenger. I could hardly bear to look, then the online alert sounded. She was there. A moment later a box containing her instant message popped onto my screen.

"You're home." She typed in an elegant font. I typed in sensible Arial.

Thanking the cybergods, I replied, "You waited for me! Thank you."

"I got your e-mail. Both of them. So I came by on the off chance."

I felt my cheeks color. "I was worried you hadn't got the first one."

"Were you on a date?"

"Not exactly. Just someone I met."

"Ah."

The honorable course seemed the best. "I placed a personal ad a while ago," I typed reluctantly. "Before we met."

"Is she cute?"

"She was nice. But not my type."

"What is your type?"

I thought of Eric. Self-assured. Well informed. Sexy. Funny. Cynical. Good-looking. "I don't think I have a type."

She said, "You'll have to do better than that."

"OK. Older than me and likes herself."

Reverie said, "Damn. Phone. BRB."

I ran to the bathroom then ran back. I didn't miss a thing. She was still away. I typed, "Anyway, I'm not seeing her again. We had a few drinks. That's all."

After a moment some words appeared. "You don't have to explain."

I tried to imagine how I would feel if Reverie told me she was dating. My stomach bunched. "Are you seeing anyone?" I asked.

"I told you. I gave up girlfriends for Lent."

"This is so weird," I blurted. "I think I'd be really jealous if you were."

She said, "I should hope so. You're meant to be putty in my hands."

I laughed. She had no idea how true that was. "You say that to all the girls."

"Yes. Your point?"

I stared at the letters on the screen. My fingers slowly depressed the keys. "Let's meet, Reverie."

"And spoil a beautiful friendship?"

Her flippant edge frustrated me. She evaded every attempt I made to shift our connection into real time. We still did not know one another's names.

"Why should it?" I asked. "We're still us."

"Because this is our own safe little room. We can say anything to one another in here. It's not the same in the real world. Out there we have our masks on."

"What does your mask look like."

"Most people think the angels skipped me when they were topping up the milk of human kindness."

I wasn't buying. "You can't seriously believe meeting face-to-face would destroy our friendship?"

"I don't want to take that chance. I like this. I like us."

"I like us too." I stepped back from pressuring her and told myself she was right. It would be madness to risk a very happy Net friendship on the off chance that we would hit it off in the real world.

"I don't know about you," she said. "But if I just wanted a weekend in Portland, I'd take someone I didn't care about kissing good-bye."

I tried not to cuss. I wanted to type: *I'd damn near settle for a weekend in Portland.* Instead, I said, "Last night I dreamed I was swimming and someone was watching me on the opposite shore. I'm not sure why, but I thought it was you."

A thoughtful pause followed this disclosure. "A body of water. That's the unconscious or emotions. Swimming could mean change, rebirth, starting again. Or getting to know yourself."

Dreams were an interest of Reverie's. She said she did a lot of her work there.

"It was a good dream," I said. "Although I don't think I ever made it to the shore."

"You didn't have to," she said. "You were happy just knowing someone was out there watching over you."

❖

"I offer marriage and this is how she thanks me," Eric smacked a theatrical hand to his brow.

He wanted me to go with him to his family's home near San Diego and pretend to be his fiancée. He imagined the news of our impending nuptials would prompt his father to regain consciousness and their family would be reconciled like long-lost relatives in a talk-show miracle.

Picturing his mother buying a fancy outfit for a wedding that would never happen, I poured cold water on this fantasy. "But what about when there's no big day?"

"We'll say we changed our minds. People break off engagements all the time."

"But your parents know you're gay. They're not going to buy this."

"That's where you're wrong. People believe what they want to believe." He took my hand. His expression was one of grave sincerity. "I respect your scruples. I know this is morally wrong and politically unsound and utterly contemptible, but I love my father and I want him to die with peace of mind. Is that a crime?"

He was so convincing, I found myself creating justifications of my own. Surely it could do no harm to let his dad die happy. In some alternative reality we might have been two straight people who fell in love and decided to get married, then realized we weren't meant for one another. It happened.

I took in the sensual line of his mouth, the droop of his eyelids, the careless grace of his body. A straight woman would have no trouble pretending to be besotted with Eric. I pounced on this concept. "What about your fag hags? Can't you ask one of them?"

Eric winced. "I'd rather eat a dog turd."

He painted a scary picture for me. They turn up at his mom's town apartment, the fake fiancée flashing a fake diamond. Next minute she and Mom have it all worked out. Why wait, when they could hold the wedding ceremony at Dad's bedside? Who needs a honeymoon in Hawaii when there's the beach house in La Jolla? *You never told me your folks had a beach house in La Jolla,* the fag hag squeals.

"Do you think I'd get that ring off her finger without a fight?" Eric sighed. "Mom would never speak to me again if I dumped the perfect daughter-in-law."

I could see his point. "I'll think about it."

As if sensing my waning resolve, he said, "It's not just for me, Chance. It's for you too."

"I don't understand."

"If you want a different life you have to say yes to the Fates."

"The Fates aren't asking. You are."

He placed his cheek against mine and whispered, "I promise you can wear the pants."

I elbowed him away, resenting that a man had the power to make my nipples hard. It was very confusing. "I can't take time off my job."

"Try," he begged. "You know you want to."

"Is there a computer at your mom's?"

"I knew it!" He kissed my hands.

I took them back. My fingers got enough slobbering from dogs. "I haven't said yes."

"You will."

"Last-word junkie," I grumbled.

CHAPTER SIX

L a Jolla is absurdly clean. Struck by the pristine pavements, trimmed hedges, and vast pastel bungalows, I said. "It looks like a theme park for rich people."

Eric glanced at me over his sunglasses. "You think this is pretentious? Wait till you see my parents' place."

We passed a line of faux Spanish *castillos* screened by wrought-iron fences and lush foliage. One place had white peacocks prowling the emerald lawns. It made a change from Dobermans.

"Wow." I was enthralled. "Was that Marlon Brando's house?"

"You sound like a tourist."

"I am a tourist!" I had already planned my week. The San Diego Zoo. Sea World. Old Town. Balboa Park.

We entered a curved driveway lined with heavy-headed palms. Sprinklers made rainbows above sweeping flower borders. The house was a mansion in flamingo pink stucco. Marble lions sprawled on either side of the entrance, lambs sitting between their paws.

Confounded by this display of metaphor and the opulent surroundings, I said, "You never told me your parents were bloated capitalists."

"I didn't think it was important, comrade." Eric parked the BMW he'd rented for our trip—his prized vintage Packard being too divine to be subjected to the lengthy journey from San Francisco. He got out and opened the passenger door for me, taking my elbow as I clambered out.

Crossing the terra-cotta expanse in front of the house, I felt ridiculous in the outfit he had chosen for me—butter yellow Capri pants, turquoise crop top, and sling-back sandals. I couldn't stop twisting the hefty "engagement" ring he had given me to seal our lie.

A woman descended the half-moon front steps to greet us. Dark blue eyes that might have been Eric's stared from a polished Grace Kelly face framed with ash blonde waves. She smiled coolly and ran a smoothing hand over her plain beige dress.

"I'm so very glad you could come," she said.

Eric kissed her on each cheek and introduced me like a high school boy with his prom date. "Mother, I'd like you to meet my fiancée, Chantelle Delaney."

Mrs. Standish took my hand and planted a dry little kiss on my cheek. She wore a subtle floral scent. "Welcome to our home, Chantelle," she said in a brittle tone and released me immediately.

She took Eric by the arm and we walked into an entrance hall that belonged in a movie. Remembering Suzie's advice about things you can't go wrong saying, I gazed around and said, "What a beautiful home you have, Mrs. Standish."

"Thank you." Her tone thawed slightly. "I'm afraid I can't take all the credit. My husband's passion for the beaux arts has always defined our living spaces."

What to say to a woman who channeled *Architectural Digest*? "I can see how much time and thought went into this," I declared with suitable awe. "The artworks alone. Breathtaking."

A little more of the permafreeze melted. "My dear, you must be desperate to freshen up." With the faintest hint of coyness, she reached for my left hand. "But first, let me see it."

My heart almost stopped beating. Here was a woman who knew what real diamonds looked like. We were doomed. I smiled with rabbity eagerness and exclaimed, "Isn't it totally perfect?"

"A wonderful choice," she agreed. "I love the Asscher cut...that tranquil pool effect."

Eric took this endorsement in stride. "I couldn't resist. It was between an Asscher and a radiant."

"A radiant..." In a hush-hush tone, Mrs. Standish confided, "Rather Hollywood, don't you think? What do they call it? Oh, yes... *bling*—dear me."

"Mother, you are such a snob. But you're right. A classic cut suits Chantelle best."

She nodded intently. "You were wise to go under three carats." As if I weren't standing right there being discussed, she continued, "Anything larger would look vulgar on a hand like hers. And the platinum is ideal for her skin tone."

I was impressed. Eric must have paid quite a lot of money for a fake that would fool a connoisseur like his mother. I called to mind what a fag hag might say in a situation like this, and gushed, "That's exactly what I thought too. I just couldn't believe it when he proposed."

"I think we were all surprised," Mrs. Standish said dryly.

She summoned a solidly built maid, who picked up my bags, ordered Eric to bring his, and led us to an upstairs room with views of the sea. There was one bed.

"I thought you said we'd be in separate rooms," I hissed, when we were finally alone with our luggage. Assailed by mental images of Mrs. Standish and the maid inspecting our sheets the next morning, I bemoaned, "This is a huge mistake."

Eric shrugged off my fears. "Chill, sweetie. There are four more bedrooms on this level. I'll take one of them. No one will notice a thing."

"Are you crazy? That maid tells your mother everything, trust me."

"Maria's okay," he said. "She's been with us forever."

I rolled my eyes. About some things males had *no* idea. "I must have lost my mind agreeing to this farce. Your mother's no fool. She'll see straight through us."

"Not if we convince her we're in love. How hard can it be?"

Clearly he had no idea what women said to each other when men were not around. I was going to be grilled on every detail of our supposed love affair. And if my story didn't match his…"We need to go over the details again," I said, panicking.

"We met at our friend Suzie's birthday party six months ago and hit it off right away," Eric said.

"Yes." I picked up the story of our bogus courtship. "Then we started dating. Movies, the opera, romantic walks."

"I proposed a month ago, just before I heard about Dad."

"We were on the pier at Fisherman's Wharf," I completed. "You put the ring on my finger and said, 'Marry me or I'll go back to England with a broken heart and have to return the ring for half price.'"

"Satisfied?" he asked.

I nodded but I was unable to shake off a feeling of doom. "Your family knows you're gay. They'll never buy this."

"They've always wanted to believe it was just a phase. Mother tells all her friends I'm bisexual." Eric took my arm and steered me toward the door. "It could be worse. We could be straight and doing this for real."

I cast a departing glance around our pre-honeymoon suite. "Where's the computer?"

"She'll survive for twenty-four hours without you." Eric knew all about Reverie and said "she" was probably a cable guy with a big gut and a comb-over. I didn't bother arguing.

"I know, but I also have client e-mails to deal with. My job isn't like yours. I don't own shares in the company."

He gave me an unusually dark look and we started walking. "It wasn't my choice to leech off the family firm. But an MBA from Chicago doesn't cut it if you're a faggot, at least not according to my esteemed pater. He threw me out."

"Well, maybe things will change when…" I foundered. It seemed déclassé to imply that Eric might be able to take over the company when his father died, if that's what he wanted.

Morosely, he said, "I'm sure the old man's already thought about that."

"What do you mean?"

"I'm being realistic. I doubt he sees me as the next chairman of Standish Industrial."

I abandoned good taste. "Do you know what's in his will?"

"I have a fair idea."

"Well, he's crazy if he cuts you out of the business." I thought Eric would look fabulous in a three-piece suit, ordering executives around.

"He never forgave me for not playing football in high school," Eric mused sadly as we strolled along a pale hallway that dripped with art and costly furniture. "And I made it worse by singing in the choir instead of trying out for track."

He subsided into gloomy silence. We shared a similar history when it came to sports. We'd both missed getting on every team, and we'd both ended up fucking the jocks who made captain. I thought about Helga Caldwell, my second lover and the best soccer player at my school.

These days my one-time tutor in advanced oral sex technique was married to a Christian conservative and organized pro-fetus fundraisers. But I happened to know she also snuck out to lesbian venues to engage in anonymous sex every time hubby was out of town.

She'd hit on me once during this self-abasing quest for gratification, and poured out her story when she sobered up enough to recognize who I was. I told her she didn't have to live a lie, but she had three kids and her husband had political ambitions. Hypocrisy was a necessary expedience.

I touched Eric's hand. "Don't worry. He'll take one look at us and realize he's made a big mistake. I'm sure he'll totally buy it."

Eric sighed. "I hope so. It would be great, for once in my life, not to disappoint him."

❖

I tried to persuade myself that the worst was over after our first dinner with Eric's mother. But nothing could have prepared me for breakfast the next morning. Eric and I went downstairs, smoochily holding hands for the benefit of all and sundry. We paused a few yards from the breakfast room, collecting our wits.

"Remember," he said. "Tender glances." He pushed open the door and we were onstage.

Mrs. Standish was sitting in an armchair before a wall of French doors that opened onto a vast terra-cotta patio. She looked up from her *New York Times* and greeted us without a glimmer of suspicion. It took me several seconds to realize she was not alone, and then I found myself staring at the most drop-dead-gorgeous woman I had ever seen. Her hair was dark and straight like Eric's. It fell just below chin level and was cut blunt like an old-fashioned schoolgirl's. I decided she was a cross between Lolita and Circe. My mom had a pre-Raphaelite print of that legendary temptress on the wall of her guest room. It could have been a portrait of the woman I was now ogling.

"Layla!" Eric discarded my hand like it was a baby diaper. "When did you get here?"

"About half an hour ago." She rose from her chair, arms outstretched. "It's great to see you, and—" Her languid gaze shifted to me, making my skin hot.

"Chantelle," Eric supplied and hastily reached for my hand once more, drawing me to his side. For the first time since we'd arrived I caught a flash of shame in his expression. "Darling, this is my cousin Layla Wilde. We virtually grew up together. She's the songwriter. Remember?"

Not even slightly. "Of course."

I was vaguely aware of him chattering about her success, of Mrs. Standish looking on, reserved but indulgent. A brilliant ocean seemed to flood the room, drowning out all sounds but for the thud of my heart in my ears. As though tangled in seaweed, my legs refused to move. I held my breath, willing myself to surface. It was *she*, the mermaid whose siren song had drifted on trade winds until the merest whisper reached me in my bed night after night, reminding me she was out there somewhere, yearning just as I was. It was the ghostly impression of her face I had seen in Eric that first enchanting moment when I mistook him for a woman.

She was speaking to me. I had no idea what she was saying. She might have been using another language.

"Excuse me?" I stammered, attracting a strange look from Mrs. Standish.

Layla tilted her head to one side and a swish of fine jet-black hair moved against her cheek. Her ears were perfect and adorned only with small, glittering crimson studs. Rubies, perhaps. She was uncannily like Eric.

"I was being nosey," she said in a voice so soft and lyrical it could only belong to a goddess.

I wanted to touch her throat. The skin was like the proverbial lilies. I could imagine color washing and receding as it was stroked. I could imagine biting into her, and finding that her veins ran with milk and honey. Someone famous had once said that about Marilyn Monroe. I knew exactly what he meant.

Eric gave me a sharp nudge. "We haven't settled on a day yet, have we, darling?"

My mouth was as dry as dust. I shook my head, feeling blood rush to my cheeks.

This earned an approving look from Mrs. Standish, who commented, "Well, what a rare pleasure it is to find a young lady who can still blush in this day and age."

"Chance was educated by nuns." Eric grinned as though letting our companions in on a private joke.

I met Layla's eyes. They were the color of cornflowers, a dark violet blue. Her beautiful mouth parted just enough so it looked like she expected to be kissed. "Chance?"

My teeth chattered. I could hardly speak. "It's a nickname—short for Chantelle."

"It suits you."

I tried to smile but all I could think about was walking her backward to the sofa and pushing her down into the pillows. Apart from that night at the bar when I mistook Eric for a woman, I wasn't sure if I'd ever lusted after anyone so intensely at first sight.

"Obviously Chantelle's parents cared about her moral and spiritual well-being," Mrs. Standish said, apparently pleased by the idea of nuns. She rang for breakfast. "I hope you have an appetite, this morning, my dear. I noticed you barely ate last night."

I nodded weakly and said something about car trips and food. The thought of eating made me even queasier than did Layla's unflinching gaze.

I have no idea what we consumed. All I can remember is Layla peeling the furry skin from a ripe peach in a long, circular strip and sliding the dripping fruit, one slice at a time, into her mouth. This was a first; I had never been envious of produce in my life.

After breakfast, Eric and his mother went to the hospital. I was to accompany them on a later visit, provided everything "went well." I chose a socially acceptable book from the selection Eric and I had brought along, and retreated to a deck-chair by the swimming pool. I had been there just a few minutes when Layla strolled along the Italianate tiles toward me.

She was carrying a brightly colored hold-all bag and had exchanged her breakfast outfit for a thin white cotton shirt tucked into a pair of khaki shorts with the hems rolled up. These displayed firm, slender legs that seemed long for her height, and through the clinging cotton of her shirt, I detected two dark little bumps pressing against the fabric. Immediately, I dismissed the happy thought that her body had reacted to me. Some women always had hard nipples. Before I could stop myself,

I stole a glance at my own, which were suddenly tight and sore.

I realized then that Layla was watching me intently, a fact that made me extremely self-conscious. The corners of her mouth twitched and, indicating the deck chair next to mine, she asked, "Mind if I join you?"

I shrugged and longed for a fraction of her poise. What must she think of me, sitting there, my lips refusing to release more than a small murmur?

As though there was nothing unusual about my staring and mumbling, she sat down and unfurled a *Vanity Fair* magazine. Taking a pair of sunglasses from her pocket, she said, "I've asked Maria to bring us some iced tea. I don't know about you, but I find waiting very tedious."

"Waiting?"

She slid the sunglasses on. "For Uncle James to die. I know it sounds callous, but I can't claim feelings I don't have. It's Aunt Patricia who's blood kin. She's my mother's twin sister."

"No wonder you and Eric are so alike."

"Yes. We could almost be twins ourselves." She let her glasses slide down her nose slightly and her pansy dark eyes regarded me from over the designer frames. "Did Eric tell you we were born the same year?"

"No. He didn't mention that."

"What exactly has he told you about me?"

I wasn't sure what she was asking. "Very little," I said in a noncommittal tone.

"Well, he's told me nothing about *you*. The engagement came as quite a shock, actually." There was an edge to her voice.

"It *was* pretty sudden, but you know how it is. We just got kind of swept away." This was one of the rebuttals Eric and I had rehearsed. It sounded even phonier now.

"How did you meet?"

"At a friend's birthday party a few months ago." So far, so good. "We got talking, and…"

I became intensely conscious of her thighs, sleek and beautifully shaped below the hemline of her shorts. Blood infused my tender places and made them throb with awareness—my nipples, the inside of my bottom lip, my clit and the rapidly swelling zone around it. I was thankful to be sitting down so my knees could only buckle figuratively.

"Now I've embarrassed you." That kiss-me smile once more. "I guess it's been pretty hot and heavy, huh?"

I looked away and shifted awkwardly in my chair, damp panties causing me a problem. Layla stared at me and I saw a flash of comprehension.

"Oh my God." She slapped her magazine closed and cast it to one side. "You're not saving yourself for the wedding night, are you?" Apparently reading my horrified silence as assent, she was suddenly deadly serious, her little round sunglasses perched halfway down her nose. "Look, I'm sorry, but I have to ask this. Have you and Eric slept together?"

I managed to find my voice. It came out as an indignant squeak. "I don't think that's any of your business." I slid my feet to the ground, signaling my desire to end this sordid conversation. But before I could get my shaky legs to support my weight, she all but shoved me back into my chair.

"Wait! Chance, please. I apologize." She waved past me to someone. "Look, here come our drinks."

We were both silent as Maria placed a pitcher and glasses on the table beside us. I could guess what Layla was thinking. She had to know Eric was gay, and she obviously assumed I had no idea, which could only mean that I was a naïve dupe he'd conned into a marriage of convenience. I permitted myself a moment of self-congratulation. Clearly I'd played my part in this charade brilliantly.

Layla flicked a sharp sideways glance at me. I could tell she was longing to question me some more, but she made a show of opening her magazine instead. As she read, I surreptitiously devoured the outline of her breasts beneath her shirt. Something told me I was staring at an opportunity. I frowned in concentration. What had the Fates delivered?

Abruptly, she lifted her head. In a tone that was carefully neutral, she said, "Eric mentioned you plan to visit the zoo tomorrow. I wondered if you'd mind some company?"

I did not fall on my knees and thank God. Instead I said blandly, "Sure, why not?"

❖

"Terrific. Now you tell me." I agonized to Eric later that evening after a truly hair-raising dinner. "*She's* gay and she knows *you're* gay. Is it any wonder she's suspicious?"

"You haven't told her what we're doing, have you?" he said, alarmed. "She'd be on the phone to Aunt Sara in a New York minute, and that's as good as telling my mother."

"Calm down." I tried not to dwell on the fact that Layla was a lesbian. She thought I was straight, and for Eric's sake I had to make sure it stayed that way. "I haven't breathed a word and I really don't think she's sprung me."

"You're a good actress."

"Yeah, who knew I could pass for straight so easily?" I grumbled. "As a matter of fact, your cousin thinks I'm a poor infatuated virgin you've conned into a loveless marriage for the sake of appearances."

Eric's mouth twitched. "How droll."

"I'm glad you think it's funny. How's your father, anyway?"

"Still unconscious." There was a note of grief. "Mom told him about us."

"And?" I gelled my hair, determined to flatten the wayward tuft into submission. I wondered if I should tape it down overnight, so it would behave on tomorrow's zoo expedition.

Eric said, "I don't know if it was my imagination, but I sensed something. And there was a flutter. I was holding his hand."

"You think he's going to wake up?"

"I'm going to spend the day there tomorrow. Just me and him."

While I'm at the zoo, I thought happily. Just me and Layla. "Good idea," I said.

"I want you to know I'm really grateful to you. For everything. You're a real friend."

"Remember that next time we're downloading from iTunes, rich boy."

He kissed my cheek. "Want me to show you the computer?"

"Sure."

I felt like a jerk as Eric led me along an airy hallway. I hadn't chatted with Reverie for two days. That's not what made me feel bad. I had told her I was going away and that I might be offline. The trouble was, I hadn't thought about her all day. What did it mean? Was I shallow? Had our connection suddenly evaporated because I had a real woman on the brain now?

Eric had installed dialup and Messenger on the computer. His mom didn't understand the Internet. I knew that before he told me. She was the kind of woman who didn't understand why people shopped in Wal-Mart, either.

"What's your friend's time zone?" he asked.

"I'm not sure. Her profile says California."

"So she could live in Russia for all you know?"

"She's not a foreigner." Some things you can tell.

"If she's local and she doesn't have anything to hide, why won't she meet you?"

"She likes us the way we are."

"Guys I've met online—they'll hook up the next day. Or that night if they live close by."

"That's because you're only looking for sex, so it's just a transaction. You don't need to spend time getting to know each other."

Eric looked unrepentant. "Well, a good fuck can be hard to find and when you do, let's just say both parties are appreciative."

"My point exactly. It's all you care about."

"Hey. I've tried romantic personal ads. I've done deep and meaningful. You should have seen the last liar I was fooled into meeting. We are talking five two, micro-wiener, bad breath, and a toupee."

I said, "Reverie isn't a liar."

"You've been talking to her for months," he marveled. "If you're so sure, isn't it time to take it to the next level?"

I didn't want to admit that I'd given up asking her to meet face-to-face. I was trying to trust that one day she would be ready. "The time has to be right for us both," I said lamely.

"Whatever you say." He keyed a password into the computer and pulled the chair out for me, "It's all yours."

I sat down. "Don't worry. I'm not kidding myself about anything."

With just a hint of irony, Eric said, "Well, that's a relief."

❖

Reverie came online about twenty minutes later. As always, my heart leapt and my fingers trembled on the keyboard. "Hey," I typed. "How are you?"

"I missed you," she said. "It was weird. Like suddenly being unanchored."

So, she'd noticed the disconnect too. I was pleased about that, but also a little unnerved. I didn't want to suggest that the dissipation of our usual connectedness was any more than an anomaly, so I said, "Well, I'm here now."

"Are you seeing someone?"

"No," I denied instantly. "I'm just on vacation."

"They're not mutually exclusive."

"Are you jealous?" Joy clamored like bugs beneath my skin, making me completely spastic at the keyboard. After all this time, could Reverie be the one who felt vulnerable for a change? I was thrilled, my feeling of distance instantly erased.

A long pause. "Possibly."

I typed some jumbled words, then backspaced over them and keyed, "I would tell you if I met someone."

"Are you still trying? I thought you'd given up on the personals."

"I have. How about you?"

"I went on a blind date last week."

I missed a breath. "You didn't tell me."

"It wasn't going anywhere, so I didn't think it was important."

After all these months of turning me down, she'd been willing to meet a stranger face-to-face? A person who was *nothing* to her! Tears stung my eyes. I couldn't type. I was insanely jealous. How had she met this woman? Did she have another online flirtation happening? Had she chosen some slick operator over me?

When I didn't type anything for a while, she said, "Faith, please don't be upset. An old friend set us up. I just thought I should go along with it so she didn't feel hurt."

Could I believe her? She could say anything and I'd have no way of knowing if it was true or not. I said flatly, "I want your phone number. It's time we talked."

"I need to think about that."

What was new? "No, you need to call me." I typed my cell phone number on the screen, not for the first time. "Please. This is not making any sense to me."

"Why do I get the feeling I'll never see you again if I refuse?"

"Probably because it's true." I could feel myself getting worked up and dramatic, another tendency of mine that puts women off. The keys clattered beneath my fingers as I banged out, "We can't keep doing this forever. I need to be able to believe you're real, but you won't let me. I want your photo. I want to talk to you. Aren't you sick of just talking in a box on a screen? Aren't you curious too?"

"Of course. But I'm also a realist. One of the things that makes *us* work is that we don't have to deal with real time, don't you see that?"

I tried to be patient. I knew where she was coming from. We'd talked about the strange magic of our connection—how we knew when the other one was online, how we had a feeling when there was an e-mail waiting. How ecstatic we were to see one another's names light up. We'd agreed that this weird morphic resonance we called our "version of love" was better than none at all.

I said, "I know you're afraid that if we see each other and it doesn't work, it'll spoil everything. But what if that doesn't happen? What if we're just as good in real time as we are on the computer? Wouldn't it be worth finding out?"

"So we gamble what we actually have, which is perfect in its own way, against the mere possibility of something better? I'm not sure if I want to do that."

Yet again, it occurred to me that Reverie was just living out a fantasy, being a lesbian in her spare time online. "Are you married?" I asked. "Please. Just tell me the truth. Are you even a lesbian?"

"I'm queer and I'm not married," she said. "What about you. Got a husband? A boyfriend?"

I stared down at my mock engagement ring and told myself this farce would be impossible to explain. Anyway, it was only a temporary situation and not for real, so I didn't feel bad about saying, "There's no boyfriend. I've been a lesbian my whole life."

"And you're really, truly single?" she asked.

"You can phone my best friend and ask her if you want." Suzie didn't know much about Reverie. I'd been too embarrassed to tell her that I'd been opting out of things we would normally do together so that I could keep chat dates with a woman I'd never seen. But I knew Suzie would vouch for me if anyone ever wanted to know about my status.

"That won't be necessary," Reverie said. "I trust you."

I said, "What about you? When was your last serious relationship?"

"I broke up almost two years ago." It was the same story she'd told early in our online friendship.

"How come you broke up?" This was the part she hadn't shared.

She left the screen blank for an eternity. "It just didn't work out and I stopped loving her."

That seemed pretty normal. Her lack of trust and paranoia about exchanging photos had made me wonder if she actually had an obsessively jealous partner and a secret life online. "So it's all past history and now you're going on blind dates." I felt angry again. "I'm not getting what the problem is about meeting me in person. Is it looks?"

I tried to imagine Reverie disfigured in some way. Less than perfect. Would it change how I felt about her? Maybe, I conceded, feeling like a terrible person. Without a photograph, I'd constructed my own image of a pale-haired beauty wearing a flimsy little dress, pearl necklace, and ballet shoes. I wasn't even sure if I found that persona attractive. How I'd felt about Reverie, ever since we started chatting, was weirdly besotted. I needed to see her. She made me laugh and she made me see that anything was possible. My world was expanded with her leaning against the front door frame of my mind, kissing me good-bye and good luck as I ventured into the unknown.

She said, "I've told you how I look. Ordinary."

"If it's no big deal, then send me a photograph."

For a long while she didn't respond, then a box popped up announcing an incoming file transfer. I broke into a sweat. Expecting a trick, maybe a picture of a cute kitten, I saved the jpeg, wiped my damp forehead against my arm, and clicked on "open file."

"I just took it," Reverie said, and sure enough there she was, sitting in front of a computer with our chat screen in the center.

The focus wasn't exactly crisp; she must have held the camera away from her and clicked. But I could see a small, sweet, face with a chin that was more pointed than round. She had golden blonde hair cropped close—the kind of style you could only get away with if your head was a perfect shape. Hers was. Bright, slightly almond-shaped eyes shone at me from beneath dead straight eyebrows that made her expression seem graver than it really was. She was smiling a cautious, uneasy smile like she was uncomfortable facing the camera. Her top lip was thin, a delicate bow over a much fuller bottom lip. Her nose was exactly right for her face, narrow and slightly on the long side. I couldn't tell her eye color, but it looked brown.

She wasn't a Layla, whose beauty came as a shock and made her seem somehow unapproachable. Reverie looked real and far from ordinary. Elfin. A little boho in her dress. Shy and sexy. She looked exactly like she seemed in chat. I wanted to meet her in the worst way.

I said, "Thanks for the pic. You're really beautiful. I don't have one of me on this computer, but when I get home I'll send it. Okay?"

"Only if you want to," she said.

I detected a trace of censure and knew I'd pressured her, but we'd done things her way for months. Surely it was time for a compromise that was less one-sided. Pushing my luck a little, I said, "Of course I want to, and then I want us to meet."

I could almost hear her sigh. "Can't photos be enough?"

I didn't want to sound churlish so I said, "I'm really happy to see your face. It means a lot."

"But?"

"Please tell me your real name. Mine is Chance Delaney."

The screen stayed blank for ages, until finally, she said, "I wish you hadn't done that."

I sighed with frustration. I'd told her my first name weeks earlier, without her having to ask. I thought she'd give me hers in response, but she'd just trotted out the usual feeble excuses and refused. Then she continued calling me "Faith," as if she didn't want to use my real name.

"We're not strangers anymore," I said. "We've been talking for months."

"I think I should go," she said.

I panicked for a brief second, wondering what "go" meant. That was why I hated this shit and wanted an address and phone number, not just a date and time for our next appointment in the nebula.

"Wait," I begged.

"I'm here."

I floundered, afraid to sign off in case I never saw her name pop up again. "I didn't mean to pressure you."

"Okay."

"Please just promise me you'll think about it."

"About meeting?"

"Yes."

A pause. "I have thought about it, and I can't."

Can't? "Why not?"

"Look, we can't keep having this conversation over and over. It's ruining everything."

"What's ruining everything is your irrational fear!" I pressed "Enter" before I could stop myself.

"In that case, maybe it's better if we don't talk anymore."

"No. Reverie, I didn't mean it that way." I was so aggravated, trying to type what I felt, that my sentence was all dyslexic. I wanted her to hear my tone, to look me in the eye and tell me she didn't trust me enough for us to meet for coffee. I cursed that I did not have a photo to exchange.

"Please don't go," I pleaded.

"I think we should say good-bye." There was a horrible finality about her words.

"I disagree."

"It's been great," she continued. "But sooner or later this always happens. Don't feel bad. I wish I hadn't sent the pic now."

Fuck! I felt like shit. "Let's chill and talk about it in a few days. Okay?"

"Okay. I'll e-mail you."

I didn't believe a single, glib word. "Let's just log on Friday night as usual."

"Sure. Bye, Chance. Be happy."

Finally, she'd called me by name. I felt no joy. In fact, with a sinking certainty, I knew I would not see her again. "You too, Reverie," I said, hating my helplessness. "I'll be here Friday."

In the IM box, a little yellow smiley face popped up, then she was gone. I wanted to swat the smug emoticon right off my screen. Miserable, I closed Messenger and was left staring at her pic, wondering how I could have handled this better. Her pixel self stared back, and for the first time I saw the accusation in her eyes.

She had wanted things to be different. I had no idea why she wasn't ready to give me her name and meet me in the flesh, and now, by forcing her hand, I'd shown that I could not respect her wishes. I didn't trust that she had her reasons and that they might not be about me. Was this something I did with other women? Was this one of the reasons I got dumped? My head hurt, thinking about it.

I turned off the computer and slouched back to my bedroom like it was Halloween and a big kid just stole my candy. I had hoped that by becoming a more interesting person I'd be the perfect mate for a smart, cute woman like Reverie. Evidently, I'd underestimated my failings. If I wanted to become half of a successful happy couple, I would have to learn how to give my partner what she truly wanted. To do that, I would have to discover who she really was and love her enough that her happiness mattered to me as much as my own.

Love was unselfish. I finally understood what that really meant. It wasn't about paying for the drinks.

CHAPTER SEVEN

With Layla beside me, even the baboons looked adorable. Their scabby pink asses did not make me squirm. Instead I saw Mother Nature at work, splendid in her diversity. I felt enriched. I loved the way Layla studied these captive creatures, her expression brimming with awe. I loved how she respected their dignity and space, standing well back from the enclosure.

"Don't—" She touched my arm as I started to move closer. "They spit twenty feet."

Covertly, I admired the smooth line of her jaw, the hollow at the base of her throat, the slope of her shoulders. She caught me looking.

Making like I was about to ask her something, I said, "How do you write your songs. I mean, do you start with the music or the words, or what?"

"I start with a feeling, then—" A slight frown puckered the bridge of her nose. "It's like there's a part of my brain that only functions when I write music. It just seems to take over." She gave me a playful look. "I suppose you're thinking, now she's gonna say she hears voices, right?"

Wrong. I was thinking: *Take me.* I made a noise that was meant to be a sophisticated chuckle. One of the baboons in the enclosure looked at me like I was the exhibit.

"No, I was thinking it must be great to have a gift like that," I said feebly.

"You're putting me on."

"Not at all."

She was all grins. "I can take it." She slid her arm into mine and started walking. "So tell me, what do you think about when you're shaving poodles?"

Be cool, I told myself as her body brushed mine. "Food, mostly," I confessed, totally blowing it. Why not wear a button that said *Dweeb*?

We stopped at the gorilla enclosure to peer hopefully through gaps in the tropical foliage.

"Isn't this fantastic?" Layla said. "Zoos have come a long way."

I nodded, suppressing nostalgia for the bad old days when the animal was completely exposed in a spartan cage and you could stare all you wanted.

"It breaks my heart to think of these noble creatures deprived of their homes because human beings are so greedy and destructive." Her voice trembled. "Fifty species a day are being wiped out so we can have mahogany furniture and eat hamburger. How disgusting is that?"

Suzie and I had this conversation every time we ate out. She refused to set foot in a Burger King. "I've been thinking about going vegetarian," I said. It was almost true. I'd been right off bacon since *Babe*.

Layla squeezed my arm. "You'll feel much better. I guarantee it." She hadn't eaten meat since high school, she told me as we passed the aviary on our way to the orangutans. "I guess you had no choice what you ate at the convent."

"It wasn't exactly a convent," I said, anxious to correct the impression Eric had given.

I wasn't sure why Mom had refused to allow me to go to the local public school after we moved to Eureka. My grandparents had pressured her, I supposed, and back then, she was very Catholic. She also wanted to punish my father for the divorce by making him pay for an expensive prep school. So the lawyers had claimed I could not be educated locally since my mother was now forced to return to a demanding career instead of being a home-maker, and I was duly dispatched to Flintridge Sacred Heart Academy near Pasadena.

Despite the fact that the school was run by the Dominican sisters, not the most liberal of orders, I did not occupy the dank little cell Layla seemed to envision. Our boarding accommodations were located in what had once been a luxury hotel patronized by rich bootleggers and industrialists. The sisters had bought it for a song after the great 1929 stock-market crash.

I said, "Nuns taught us, but they weren't as narrow minded as you might think."

"You sound defensive," she said. "I'm only curious. Your life is so different from mine."

"In what way?"

"God, where do I start?"

"How about the best day of your life," I suggested.

"It hasn't happened yet. At least I hope not." She swung a cute sideways glance at me. "I'll tell you mine, if you tell me yours."

"Sure." I had nothing to hide. My life was a sea of tedium. Choose any day and it would be much the same as another. "Your turn first," I gallantly offered.

"Okay. Picture this." She closed her eyes. "I'm in New Orleans. It's one of those sticky August nights and I'm walking in the Quarter with a frozen strawberry daiquiri in my hand. You can tell there's a storm coming. The air is just oozing. It's like swimming in warm marshmallow. Every bar on Bourbon has its wood shutters open and they're playing the best rhythm and blues you'll ever hear.

"I stop to listen to this guy playing saxophone and, maybe I'm drunk, but I start crying. He can see me there in the doorway and it's like he knows I have a broken heart and he starts to play for me. We could be the last two people on earth." She sighed. "Later on, it starts raining and I get soaked to the skin walking back to my hotel, but I don't care. I feel alive. It's magic."

I couldn't think of anything to say. I could see her, as the saxophone player might have seen her, loitering in that cramped doorway, a solitary figure painted against a backdrop of smoke and boozy laughter. I imagined her walking in the rain, bedraggled yet somehow incandescent. She could have been a nineteenth-century heroine, caught between convention and self-awareness on a journey to the passionate self. I pictured her striding across a windswept English moor, wickedly attired in men's breeches and riding boots. This vision took my breath away.

Her eyes blinked open and the pupils contracted sharply against the glare of the sun. "Chance?" She touched my arm and I ached to kiss her. "Your turn—the best day of your life."

Today, I wanted to say. This moment. You with your sexy smile and your little shorts. I scrambled desperately for a memory I could share, some captivating proof that I, too, had a meaningful life. "Mmm, the best day of my life," I stalled. "Well…"

Nearby someone's kid erupted in a tantrum, banging on the glass wall that protected the simians before collapsing on the spongy green flooring. Like everyone else, we glanced over. He was all fists and legs, about two years old, no investment in keeping up appearances. I was almost envious.

Layla moved her dark glasses back up her nose and said, "Let's go get a soda."

"Great idea," I breathed, dizzy with relief. "My treat."

❖

The house was empty when we got back. Mrs. Standish was calling on friends and Eric was still at the hospital. I went upstairs to shower and change. I did not expect to find Layla lounging on my bed in a black satin kimono when I emerged from the bathroom.

"Hey," she said like it was no big deal that I was naked and had my towel draped over my shoulder. "I knocked, but I guess you didn't hear me."

I whipped the towel down and wrapped myself in it. Determined not to blush, I forced myself to think about the smell of gasoline and the stress of cutting dog toenails.

"You know something," Layla said as I knotted the towel aggressively over my breasts. "I'm glad you're marrying Eric. I always wanted a sister, and you'll be the next best thing."

I stage-managed a smile. "I wanted a sister too."

"Funny, isn't it, that we're all only children—you, me, and Eric."

"Yes." Was I supposed to get dressed in front of her as if we were impassive strangers in a locker room? I took a shirt and jeans from the closet and draped them over the back of a chair. Layla made no move to leave.

"I'm sorry I was weird about everything yesterday by the pool." She rearranged the pillows and settled back. "Please tell me about you and Eric." Her expression was one of keyed-up expectancy, as if we were teenagers sharing secrets at a slumber party.

In my most discouraging tone, I asked, "Tell you what?"

"Oh, you know. The romantic stuff. Was it really love at first sight?"

"Pretty much." I recalled my first impression of Eric as the woman of my dreams. "I almost passed out when I saw him."

"What was he wearing?"

"Jeans. Turtleneck. Leather jacket."

"Mmn, I know that look. Eric has a certain…androgynous beauty, wouldn't you say?"

"I guess." I tried to sound clueless.

"Actually, you have something of that quality yourself, Chance." She studied me more closely.

I tried to read her face. Had she figured me out? Hoping not to convey guilt or nerves, I said, "Uh-huh," and casually gathered up my clothing, heading for the bathroom.

"Wait!" A laughing protest. "Eric leaves out all the good bits when we talk about this. Come on, Chance. Spill!"

I hovered in the bathroom doorway, wanting to escape but weirdly unable to put a closed door between us. Her expression was so sweet and coaxing and the tease of her body beneath the flimsy satin had me reduced to a state of wet, weak thrall.

"I should get dressed," I said without conviction. "Eric will be home soon."

She looked perplexed, as if it hadn't crossed her mind that I might not want to indulge in girl talk and that I might prefer to dress in privacy. Her voice dropped to a throaty tease and her face wore a distinctly come-hither expression. "You're shy," she murmured.

"No, I'm not." I knew my cheeks rosily declared this to be untrue.

"I won't look," she said with a wicked little grin. "In fact, if it would make you more comfortable, I can take this off."

To my shocked delight, she sat up and unfastened the belt of her kimono, allowing the garment to slither down her shoulders until her breasts were uncovered. Like the rest of her, they were to die for, and obviously not implants. Her small plum red nipples stood hard and expectant and her eyes challenged me to react. What was she playing at? I was her cousin's fiancée, yet she was flirting with me. It was a test, I decided. She was trying to push my buttons, trying to find out if "androgynous" meant queer in my case. Trying not to drool and give myself away, I compelled my gaze to stay riveted to a spot slightly west of her face.

With what I hoped was polite disinterest, I said, "You're welcome to wait if you want. I'll only be a few minutes." I could not draw breath. Layla was half naked on my bed and shamelessly enticing. She slid one foot slowly along the muscular arch of the calf it rested upon. The invitation was so provocative I knew if I didn't escape immediately, I'd have to touch her.

Yearning made me ache and shiver. My heart deafened me. It was all I could do not to cross the room and drop to my knees. I was ready to beg her to do with me as she pleased, to let me please her. I'd never wanted to be anyone's sex slave, but I now understood the urge.

"God, those nuns did a job on you," Layla said softly. "You're such an innocent."

"No, I'm not." It sounded like someone else's hoarse protest.

"Really?" She slid her legs over the side of the bed and stood. Drawing the kimono into place again, she tied the narrow belt. "I'm sorry. I didn't mean to embarrass you."

Rooted to the spot and alarmed by my inability to walk away, I latched on to a mundane subject. "I had a nice time at the zoo. Thanks for coming along."

Instead of strolling out of my room, Layla crossed the floor to stand a few inches from me. In bare feet, we were the same height, which meant that if I didn't slouch everything was aligned. Eyes, mouths, nipples, groins. She sized me up like she was thinking exactly the same thing. With her face just inches from mine, I could see how perfect her features were. She had the kind of cheekbones that got fashion photographers worked up, and a smooth high forehead that balanced her angular chin and jaw. Her eyes were hypnotic. Sapphire and violet glimmered from a fine webbing of black, like gems had been crushed to tint her irises. The pupils dilated as she gazed at me, consuming the color around them until it seemed her irises were black with a violet halo. She had eyelashes so ridiculously long I thought they were fake at first, but as they swept down onto her cheeks, I could see she wasn't even wearing mascara.

"Do something for me." She lifted a hand to my cheek. "Tell me how you really feel about Eric."

Her eyes locked on mine. I knew she would see right through me if I lied. Scrambling for a truth I could tell with complete sincerity, I said, "We really love each other."

Her palm smelled of daphne, a succulent sweet tang that made me imagine drifting through the groves of Delphi, seeking out the handmaidens of the Oracle. Normally, I wasn't prone to such flaky imaginings, but Layla would bring out the dreamer in anyone.

She angled her head and her face brushed mine. Her breath was warm against my ear, her lips so unbearably close I shuddered and closed my eyes. "Go get dressed," she murmured.

I turned my head just a fraction, my breathing out of control. I had to kiss her.

With a wicked little smile, she drew away just as I zoomed in on her mouth. "Are you okay? You're shaking."

Spared from totally blowing it, I stumbled back a step. Had she been merciful or was this just another level of teasing? "I'm cold," I said. "That's all."

She lifted a hand and trailed her fingertips slowly down my arm. "Mmn. You have goose bumps." Like she had no idea how *that* could have come about.

I took several guilty backward steps into the haven of the bathroom, and we stared at one another as if on opposite sides of a no-man's land we would cross at our peril.

"I can see you're all wet and uncomfortable…from your shower," she said. "I'm sorry to have kept you talking so long."

"It's okay." I reached for the door handle, signaling that the conversation was over. "I'll see you downstairs."

Before she could answer, I closed the door on her piercing gaze and her sexy smile. Layla was onto me. I knew it and she knew it.

CHAPTER EIGHT

I hate the sanitized squeak of hospital floors. I hate the tranquil facade that conceals so much pain and misery. There was a nurse in Mr. Standish's room, changing his drip. She greeted us brightly, informing us that he'd had a "comfortable night," although I could not imagine how she knew this. Mr. Standish was lying like a dead person, eyes wide open.

"He hasn't regained consciousness?" Eric asked.

The nurse shook her head. Adjusting the pillows around her patient, she raised her voice like she was talking to the deaf and announced, "Your son's here to see you, Mr. Standish."

Not a flicker.

She indicated a buzzer. "If you need anything, just press this." With a smile that excluded me, she was gone.

Mr. Standish was no one's idea of handsome. He had bushy eyebrows that met on the bridge of his nose, and his features could have belonged to a boxer. It was hard to believe he was Eric's father. The good-looks gene had evidently skipped a generation.

Eric sat down beside the bed. "I've brought Chantelle to see you, Dad."

I watched the monitoring equipment for signs of a response. But this was not a medical drama where needles jumped and wild-eyed doctors shouted for plasma.

"Say something to him," Eric whispered.

I took Mr. Standish's hand in mine. "It's good to meet you, sir. I believe you're an opera fan."

The heart monitor continued its uniform blips.

Eric said, "Chantelle adores the opera. We're going to see Renée Fleming at the Met next month." To me, he whispered, "That might wake him up. He thinks she's overrated."

I studied Mr. Standish carefully, seeking the slightest sign of a person present in the respirating body. Eric was kidding himself if he thought his father was ever going to regain consciousness.

"What do the doctors say?" I whispered. "Do they think there's any chance?"

"You know what doctors are like."

In this case, I suspected they knew more than the rest of us, but I said nothing and, after a couple more futile hours at the bedside, we drove back toward La Jolla. The more I thought about the Spanish *castillos*, and the fountains and peacocks, the more trepidation I felt. Maybe Layla had already been on the phone to her mother to share her suspicions about me. I pictured us parking the car and Mrs. Standish standing on the top step with her arms folded and her mouth set.

"I think I should go back home," I told Eric as we sat in traffic in San Diego.

"But it's only been three days."

"I can't do this." I tried to be diplomatic. "I truly hope your Dad comes 'round, but I hate lying to your family and Layla knows we're up to something."

I told him about the way she'd tested me, but he said she was like that with everyone. He warned, "Don't fall in love with her."

"Why not?"

"Because everyone does and it's completely pointless."

"Are you saying she doesn't want a girlfriend?"

"I'm saying she never chooses people who fall in love with her. I think it's too easy."

"She sounds fucked up."

"I love her, but trust me, you don't want to go there."

I said, "There's no danger of that. I know she's only trying to seduce me to prove something."

He shook his head. "No, it's not even that complicated. Layla flirts with everyone. She does it because she can. It's her version of teasing the animals."

"I don't think so," I said. "She has some kind of plan going. Maybe she's told your mother and they've hatched a scheme to catch us out."

"Layla wouldn't do that."

"Whatever. It doesn't matter. I'm not hanging around to find out. Life's too short."

"Chance, please don't go." He reached across and took my hand in his. "I want to visit him once more. Just once. Please, Chance. Will you do that for me?"

Even a lesbian can have a soft place in her heart for a man, so it pained me to remain hard. "We've done all we can do. I think you have to be realistic about this. Your dad isn't looking good."

Eric let go of my hand and drummed his fingers on the wheel. His expression was preoccupied. "I wish you'd reconsider."

We were in Old Town, all clay and pink and tourists weighed down with folk art, no doubt planning a *Spruce Goose* tour for the next day. I stared out at the weird mix of mission dwellings and seventies suburban architecture. "I don't want to lose my job."

"I could pay you."

"Are you crazy?"

He had the grace to look embarrassed. "Don't be offended."

"Too late. I did you a favor. I don't want your money."

Silence.

"Let me get something straight." I sensed there was more to his insistence than a filial desire for a deathbed blessing. "This is not just about your father, is it?"

He sighed audibly. "No. It's more complicated than that."

"You don't have to tell me," I said. "Your family is none of my business."

We reached La Jolla and drove in silence to the Standish mansion. As the electronic security gates swung open, he urged, "Just one more day. Please."

I saw Layla reclining by the swimming pool in a modest two-piece that only made her look even sexier than if she wore a thong. "Okay." I succumbed like the pitiful lust-struck fool I was. "One more day, then I'm out of here."

There was something fishy about the whole situation. Yet again, I considered Eric's motivations. Surely he didn't seriously believe his father would wake up and all would be forgiven. He had to know the odds were virtually zero. It made no sense to me that he was so much in denial. Eric wasn't stupid.

Money and sex, it was safe to assume, were at the heart of the matter. I could have pressed him for the truth, but to be honest, it suited me not to know. I didn't want something even more sordid than our sham engagement on my conscience.

❖

At dinner that night, Mrs. Standish asked me whether I planned to continue in my job after Eric and I were married.

"Of course she will," Layla said. "No one is into the happy housewife trip anymore, Aunt Patty. Women have higher expectations these days."

"How frustrating that must be for them," Mrs. Standish remarked.

Eric laughed. "Mother thinks women are worse off than ever."

I thought about Mrs. Yuppie trying to hold down her job in between throwing up every half hour. What was she trying to prove? In the same position, a man would simply go to bed and expect his partner to pander to him. Eric's mom had a point.

"Sometimes I regret not having a career," Mrs. Standish reflected. "But it's my personal belief that God did not design human beings for nine-to-five work. We are much more creative than that."

"You should have been a hippy," Eric said.

"I might have been if hippies were more interesting."

"Come on, Aunt Patty, you must have partied with the rest of them," Layla teased. "All that free love."

Mrs. Standish dismissed this notion with the contempt it deserved. "The Pill was to the sixties what Viagra is to this generation—permission to behave like fools."

"But don't you think we'd be in a very different world if it wasn't for the baby boomer generation?" Eric said. "We'd still be having the Cold War, or maybe we'd be having the nuclear winter by now."

"Free love didn't end the Cold War any more than Ronald Reagan did," Layla said dismissively. "Pragmatism did it."

"Okay, so I was being simplistic," Eric said.

"I assume you're not taking the contraceptive pill, Chantelle?" Mrs. Standish turned her laser sharp gaze my way. "Did you know most of the early Pill brands were eventually banned because of their side effects? Who knows what they'll discover about the current ones after it's too late."

Not for the first time in my life I thanked the Goddess I was a lesbian and never had to think about the sordid business of contraception. STDs were scary enough. With unflinching sincerity, I said, "No, I've never been on the Pill."

"Of course not…a Catholic girl of your upbringing. How silly of me."

Did I sense a faint perturbation mingled with the obvious approval? Mrs. Standish seemed to like the idea that I might almost be a nun, yet she had to be wondering about me and Eric. By now, the maid must have told her we weren't sharing a room. I was surprised she hadn't bailed me up in a dark corner and demanded the truth. Or had she, as I suspected, sent Layla on a fishing expedition? It couldn't be a coincidence that Eric's cousin had arrived here the day after we did.

I put myself in Mrs. Standish's shoes for a moment. Her gay son announces he's engaged and shows up with someone who doesn't look like a cheerleader. I'd certainly have my suspicions.

Eric toyed with the mint sprig in his iced tea. "Chance and I will probably want to start a family not long after we're married."

I stopped breathing, shocked to hear him lie so brazenly to his own mother. Somehow this seemed worse than any of our other lies. It was cruel and beneath him. Most mothers dreamed of grandchildren, even those who didn't seem the maternal type. It was wrong to encourage such hopes. Mrs. Standish had never done me any harm, yet I was participating in a farce that could only hurt her. Now, with one thoughtless embellishment, Eric had raised the stakes even higher.

With a disapproving frown at him, I said, "We can't make any assumptions about that, darling. Remember?"

Three pairs of eyes were riveted to me.

I produced a show of nervous mortification. "You haven't told them?"

"Er…no." Eric raised his eyebrows just enough to let me know now was a good time to stop whatever fabrication I was about to embark on.

I placed a hand on his and sighed convincingly. "I had surgery recently," I told Mrs. Standish. "For feminine problems. My doctor wasn't very optimistic."

Mrs. Standish lifted a hand to her throat. To Eric, she said, "You should have told me. Chantelle *must* see Dr. Reeves." She surveyed me more warmly than at any time since I'd arrived. "I can only imagine how upset you must be. But rest assured, you will see the very best specialists in the country. Dr. Reeves is a personal friend and a highly respected surgeon. I'll call him tomorrow."

I stared at my feet, wondering how I was going to get myself out of a hole that was getting bigger and bigger, as they do when you tell a pack of lies. This hadn't gone the way I'd planned.

Layla cut in with a protest that saved my ass. "Oh, let's not send poor Chance off to a gynecologist on her very first visit with us, Aunt Patty! She's not a brood mare."

Mrs. Standish made a sound somewhere between embarrassed laughter and irritation. "Chantelle is going to be my daughter-in-law. I only want the very best for her."

"We appreciate that," Eric said soothingly.

Clearly intending to move on from her slight faux pas, Mrs. Standish touched Layla's arm. "I was thinking, let's go shopping tomorrow. You, me, and Chantelle."

"For an engagement present?" Layla gave me a look I didn't want to fathom. "What a wonderful idea. I can hardly wait."

"I was planning to spend the day with Eric," I ventured, horrified by the prospect of playing bride-to-be on a mall crawl with my supposed future mother-in-law and a woman I wanted so badly to fuck that I thought they'd probably both hear me squelching.

Mrs. Standish turned her cool smile on me and in that moment I was certain she knew much more than she was letting on. Maybe the gynecologist suggestion had been her way of making me sweat. Could she be that Machiavellian?

"You'll have all the time in the world for Eric later on," she said.

Eric nudged me with his foot and I replied, "You're right. Shopping would be lovely."

"Eric mentioned you haven't chosen your dress because your mother has been overseas." Mrs. Standish shook her head over this incomprehensible maternal conduct. "And whilst I can respect her commitment, I'm wondering if you are aware of the issues. One cannot buy a wedding dress off the rack. I've called some friends and I have the names of a couple of couturiers we should see locally, and there's always Badgley Mischka, of course."

Aghast, I said, "Eric and I weren't planning to have the big day for a while yet, and we were thinking something simple…"

Mrs. Standish waved a hand. "My dear child, it's very sweet and romantic of you to want an understated occasion, and we'll certainly tell the wedding coordinator what we're looking for."

"The coordinator?" I prodded Eric. This was getting out of control. He needed to say something. Like, now.

"Mischka isn't right for her," he cut in, useless in the face of the deteriorating situation. "But I could see her in Vera Wang."

His mother trilled a soft laugh and regarded me warmly yet again. "I thought when I had a son, I'd never get the chance to plan a wedding, but when Eric told me about your mother, I said I would be happy to step into the breach."

"My mother?"

"It can't be helped." Eric seized my hand in his beneath the table and delivered a warning squeeze. "Mrs. Delaney made a promise to those orphans and she's not the kind of person who would go back on her word. I truly admire her for making this personal sacrifice to help the world's most vulnerable children."

"You must tell me how to donate." Mrs. Standish was patently moved. "I consider your mother's work nothing less than heroic."

"You're very kind," I said, scrambling to decipher the role now assigned to my mother in this new installment of our fictional lives.

I did not miss Layla's polite little cough. She kept her hand across her mouth and I suspected she was hiding a smirk.

"It's disappointing for Chantelle," Eric managed to sound choked up. "But at times like this we all have to look at the bigger picture."

Mrs. Standish reached out and touched my arm. "Don't worry, my dear. When your mother gets back from Eritrea, I promise you, she will be guest of honor at the most exquisite wedding La Jolla has ever seen."

Oh, God. I willed myself not to run screaming from the room. I felt like I'd entered an alternate universe. This had to end, or one day soon I'd wake up and start blathering about baby's breath versus heather, and the relative merits of wedding make-up artists.

Pasting on a brave smile, I said, "Mrs. Standish, you can't imagine what that means to me."

❖

Much later in the evening, after I'd berated Eric for letting things get out of control, I went to the library seeking solace and calm. The room seemed to belong to another house in another time. Floor-to-ceiling bookshelves. Faded rugs. Decrepit globe. Dark red leather chairs. Between these, on a low inlaid table, lay a stack of newspapers and a collection of Sylvia Plath's poetry.

I was thumbing through this, my mind guiltily on Reverie, when Layla's voice made my nipples scrape against my bra.

"Looking for some bedtime reading?"

How long had she been watching me? I returned Plath to the table and said, "I'm feeling restless."

"Me too." She occupied one of the leather chairs, tucking her feet beneath her. "On nights like this I want to be lying on a Caribbean beach staring up at the stars."

I caught her scent, a lingering musky smell unlike the light citrus fragrance she wore most of the time. She trailed a hand back and forth along the arm of her chair, apparently lost in thought, then her head lifted sharply.

"Of course!" she declared, eyes bright with purpose. "We have to swim."

I felt a sharp thrill of panic as she took my arm and hoisted me from my chair and steered me determinedly into the hall. "We won't need our bathing suits," she whispered, as if we were colluding in an escapade far more illicit than a midnight swim in her aunt's pool. "I'll turn off the floodlights."

Reluctant to be seen as a hopeless party pooper, and also too weak to say no to the prospect of Layla naked, wet, and up close, I took a couple of towels from the bathroom and crept downstairs with her.

We got undressed in the gazebo. Moonlight trickled through the latticed wood onto her body. She caught me sneaking covert glances and allowed me a closer look at a collection of silver scars on her breasts.

"I was stabbed," she said tonelessly.

I stared for the longest time, wondering how I had ended up in La Jolla, naked with this woman and what it all meant, if anything. Once upon a time I would have refused Eric's bizarre request to enter this masquerade and none of this would be happening. My life read like a laundry list of unseized opportunities. But not anymore.

Tentatively, I touched one of the scars. The air between us seemed charged with possibility. "How did it happen?"

She was slow to answer, as though selecting her words carefully. "It was a long time ago. I was…" She gave an empty laugh. "It's funny. I've rehearsed this a thousand times and I still can't say it."

I was almost scared to move, waiting for her to breathe. In her hesitance I sensed the hurt of past betrayals and I wanted to fall at her feet and promise to guard any secret of hers with passionate jealously, to share it with no one.

"It's okay," I whispered. "You can talk to me."

She sighed as though the breath had been crushed from her. "I want to. I thought I could. But…it's no good. It will never be any good."

I took her hand, reluctant to pressure her. I had learned something from my mistakes with Reverie. "Let's swim," I suggested with bright determination. "We can talk later."

We slipped quietly into the pool and floated on our backs, barely able to see one another in the darkness. Occasionally our thighs or arms collided softly and we kicked away from one another. I could feel her presence in the shifting water like proxy hands caressing my body.

I drifted to the side of the pool and stared up at the stars, wordlessly renewing my pledge to say yes to the Fates. In keeping silent during Mrs. Standish's wedding takeover bid, I had resigned from the ranks of the honest people and accepted my role in this adventure. Never again would I turn away from life's curveballs out of fear and lack of confidence. I would have courage. I would make something happen, even if the means were not ideal.

Layla emerged from the water next to me, droplets slithering down her face. "What are you thinking about?" she asked.

I hesitated, a prisoner of conflicting urges. I could make a weather comment, claim tiredness, and retreat indoors. Or I could kiss her. "I was thinking how good it is to be here." *With you*, I added mentally, not quite ready to cast all caution aside by saying so.

"Me too." She flipped onto her stomach, resting her arms and head on the handrail and keeping her body afloat with languid kicks. "I always feel safe here. It brings back happy memories."

"Eric said you and your mom lived with his family for a while when you were a kid."

"My mom didn't cope well when Dad died. Aunt Patty is the strong one."

"They say that happens with twins. That one is always the leader."

"It's like that with Mom and Aunt Patty. Mom's very intuitive. When Uncle James had his stroke she knew something was wrong and rang Aunt Patty right away."

"Is your mom coming here?"

"She's waiting until it's over."

"Mr. Standish isn't going to make it, is he?"

"It's only the machines that are keeping him alive. Poor Aunt Patty. She has to decide when to turn everything off."

This wasn't the story I'd heard from Eric. Eventual recovery. Physiotherapy to restore movement. A wheelchair. "Does Eric know this?" I asked, still puzzling over his reasons for the fake engagement. Was he just in denial?

"Yes, but it seems like he's not ready to accept it."

She started talking about Eric, remembering him as a sensitive, small boy always seeking his father's approval. I felt uncomfortable with these disclosures, shared as they were by someone who loved him with someone who was only pretending to.

"Tell me something," Layla said with a slight edge. "Are you marrying Eric for money?"

My gasp was audible. "I don't know anything about Eric's financial situation."

"I'm not accusing you," she said. "I'm curious, that's all."

I got out of the pool and sat on the edge, my towel around me. I knew my answers would be reported to Mrs. Standish. Perhaps the questions were hers too. This was when I was supposed to play the outraged fiancée and declare my undying love for Eric. Instead I said, "I'm not that kind of person."

Layla looked up at me. "What kind of person are you, Chance?"

I didn't want to get into a discussion about that, so I said, "I care about Eric."

"But you two aren't lovers, are you? How do you know the marriage is going to work?"

"Are you saying sleeping together first is some kind of guarantee that you won't get a divorce later?"

"Of course not, but it's important to know if you're compatible, don't you think?"

I decided to play a card she wouldn't be expecting. Sweetly, I said, "Eric tells me you're a lesbian, so I wouldn't expect you to understand our relationship."

She was silent for so long I wondered if she wanted to hit me and had to hold herself back. In the end, she climbed out of the pool, put on a robe and sat down next to me on the ledge. "Eric tells me *he's* gay," she countered succinctly. "So yes...I don't understand why he's marrying a woman."

In my most dignified tone, I responded, "Eric and I have spoken about his past, so if that's what you're worried about, let me reassure you. We both know exactly where we stand."

"Is he paying you to marry him?"

"What do you think I am—a prostitute?"

"I didn't say that. Chance, I'm not stupid. I know you and Eric aren't in love. So what's this all about?"

Weary of the games, fed up with trying to deceive people who could see our story wasn't hanging together, I said, "If you must know, we're not engaged anymore. It wasn't working but we agreed to wait before we ended things officially. Eric wanted to give his dad peace of mind."

"Uh-huh." Layla twiddled with the belt of her robe. "So are you telling me it *did* work for a while?"

"I love Eric. But we weren't meant to be together."

She regarded me with something akin to pity, and said, "You're the worst liar I've ever met."

I felt my throat closing. She knew. She had always known. I regretted every minute of our absurd charade. Layla must despise me. Trying for some dignity, I said, "I only ever wanted to help."

"Don't blame yourself. I confronted Eric and he admitted he was using you. Don't you see—that's why I was asking if you'd slept together."

Mystified, I repeated her comment to myself and felt rising hysteria. Had I stumbled onto the set of *Days of our Lives*? Layla only seemed to be getting half the story. Apparently, she believed I had been dumped by a gay man who had never intended to marry me. I supposed I'd just endorsed that by saying I'd agreed to keep up the engagement as a favor to him. Couldn't she see I was a lesbian? It was virtually stamped on my head.

I said, "Layla, I've known about Eric's sexuality all along."

"And you thought you could change him?" She shook her head. "Sweetheart, it doesn't work that way. He's always been gay. People are born that way." Her voice brimmed with sympathy. "You must be feeling bad about this. You don't have to pretend with me."

Bracing myself, I said, "Okay, then I won't. I do feel bad. I dislike deceit even if the reasons for it are well-meaning. But there's something else." My common sense urged me to shut up, but I said, "I'm gay too."

"Ah. So you *do* know." A pitying gaze. "I thought you didn't realize. I mean, I knew the moment I saw you, but I figured you must be getting married to avoid your feelings. Eric *is* kind of a substitute woman."

"I see." What else could I say? I lowered my head, scared I would crack up laughing. Layla had arrived at a convoluted theory to explain why two queers might decide to get married and then realize with dismay that it would never work. I supposed it was nice of her to give me the benefit of the doubt. I'd rather she thought I was just sexually confused than doing this for money.

"I've known lesbians who got married because they wanted to stay in denial," she continued with her analysis. "It's very natural. We live in a homophobic world."

"I knew it was the wrong thing to do," I said, slithering my way into the revamped rationale for my behavior. "But I didn't see the harm in trying to help Eric come to terms with his father's condition. And, I have my parents to think about too. They're always harping on about me being single."

Layla leaned across and kissed my cheek. In the moonlight, her eyes shimmered with tears. "You don't have to feel guilty. We all do stupid things when we are trying to fit in. But there's nothing wrong with being gay. If you just let yourself be who you really are, I promise you, everything will fall into place."

I bit my lip and stared down at her lissome thighs. For a moment, I wanted to laugh that she had this so right, yet so wrong. I followed the parting of her robe over the rise of her breasts to the expanse of bare skin at her throat. Water from her dripping hair slithered over her shoulders in rivulets that joined together to travel down the narrow path between her breasts. I wanted to slide my hand inside the damp cotton garment and caress her cool smooth flesh.

I wondered what Layla liked in a lover. Most of my girlfriends were orally fixated. I lifted my gaze and found her regarding me, her expression strangely mournful. Abruptly, she swung her feet up out of the water and stood with one hand extended.

"This is so public," she said. "Let's go in, Chance."

I shook my head. "You go. I need some time alone."

She didn't move, no doubt mistaking my reservations for the panic of a convent-educated woman finally confronting the scary truth that she would never be able to change her own lesbianism. I could almost hear her thought process—marrying a gay man might feel safe, but it was not going to help me. If I didn't accept myself, I would be stranded forever in one lie or another, not to mention sexually frustrated and a victim of low self-esteem. If I'd been her, I would have felt morally obligated to help me too.

Gently, tenderly, she drew me to my feet and said, "I understand exactly how you feel. But everything will be okay. Trust me?"

I let myself drink her in. I guess that was the moment when I made my choice. I knew what she was offering and I knew I should tell her she'd misunderstood a few key points. But I couldn't.

❖

We tracked back to the gazebo and showered in complicit silence. There were two private cubicles, each luxuriously appointed in what was supposed to pass for rustic outdoors décor. I soaped myself automatically, doing my best to ignore my hard nipples and the slippery parting between my thighs. Each time I brushed my clit, I winced. I hadn't had sex in months. I could be turned on by anything. A tree. Food that crunched. Any woman who looked at me twice.

As we entered the house, Layla placed her hand on my arm. She glanced around as if afraid someone might hear us. "So, how about if I come to your room for a while, so we can talk some more?"

Here was another opportunity to say no. I studied her carefully, not quite certain where things stood. Just moments ago, I'd been sure she intended to have sex with me. Now, suddenly, it seemed she might have backed off in favor of tea and sympathy. She saw me as a troubled lesbian in hiding from her true self. Maybe she'd decided to be mature and therapize me verbally instead of orally.

"Sure, come on up," I said and felt sorry for myself right away.

Wasn't it enough that I'd swum naked with a woman I craved so desperately that I needed to have an orgasm soon or I'd vandalize something? No, I had to add the refined torture of having her in my bedroom sharing confidences and being a do-gooder when I could be getting myself off.

We padded along the parquet hall to the staircase. A portrait of Mrs. Standish wearing a grotesque mock-Picasso smile hung above the landing. So much expensive modern art lined the walls that the place looked like a storage facility for the Getty Museum. Nearing my door, I told myself that saying yes to the Fates was not always such a great idea. There were times when common sense should prevail. Right now I should tell Layla I was too tired to talk. Instead, weak with longing and willing to settle for her presence under any circumstances, I let her into my room and closed the door behind us.

A single small lamp pooled amber light ineffectually into the deep shadows. I said, "Make yourself comfortable. Would you like some dry clothes?"

She shook her head and stared at me, and we moved into one another's arms as if it had been inevitable all along. I stroked her damp hair. The smell of pool chlorine kept me firmly grounded in reality. This was not a prelude to lovemaking, my doubtful self asserted. It was mere comfort. Layla thought she was helping a woman fight her way out of denial and accept herself. She was trying to be supportive and kind, even though I'd screwed around with her family.

The truth was, it didn't matter how I justified or distorted it, I craved her arms around me and not just because I desired her. I felt stressed and also needed a hug. I leaned into her and tried to keep my mind on a platonic wavelength, but that lasted for about three seconds. My towel fell to the floor and Layla's robe followed. She slid her hands into mine. In a split second, something had changed and sex was back on the table.

I rested my hot cheek against hers and worried that if I seemed too eager, Layla would lose interest like Eric had implied. "We can't do this," I said, tapping into my inner Puritan. All those years with the nuns still counted for something.

She turned her face a little, and kissed the corner of my mouth. "But you want to, don't you?"

In answer, I tilted my head just enough so that our lips met. Her warm, wet mouth welcomed mine. We tasted one another cautiously at first, then she took my tongue deep inside and her body pushed against mine. She lifted my hands to her breasts, coaxing me to cradle their soft weight. Her nipples teased my palms and I kissed her more recklessly. Her pliant flesh tightened everywhere I stroked. She slid a leg between mine. One of her hands followed and she groaned softly as her fingers connected with the wet ache I'd been trying to ignore since the moment I saw her.

I pushed my hips against her, urging her to give me what I needed. Instead she withdrew her hand and slid a finger between our two mouths, licking and sucking and kissing me at the same time, making me taste myself on her. Overcome with shock and pleasure, disbelieving that this could be happening, I kissed her until I felt dizzy. Then I lowered my head to her perfect neck and bit down slowly until I felt her shudder. At the same time, I slid one of my hands past the cool, smooth rise of her hip to cup her ass just above the thigh.

She responded by grinding her breasts and belly against mine. "I'm so wet," she murmured in my ear.

My body reacted with a renewed rush of fluid. "Come on," I croaked and we stumbled toward the bed, collapsing on the pale cotton quilt, both of us panting with desire.

I dragged her up to the pillows and leaned over her, sliding the tip of my tongue over her throat and down one irresistible breast to the pert, dark nipple. I took this between my teeth, rolling it back and forth then tenderly sucking. She moved her hands over me, stroking my head and caressing my spine. I glanced up so I could see her face. Her eyes were closed, her lips parted, her cheeks flushed. Her hair spilled across the snowy pillow in a dark angel halo.

For a moment I was awestruck, not just by her beauty which was the kind that made fools of mortals and caused the waging of wars. I was struck that she had chosen to share the wonders of herself with me. A woman like her could have anyone. Yet it was me she wanted. This seemed so unlikely and so incredible, my touch faltered and I found myself in the grip of paralyzing performance anxiety.

"Chance?" A throaty enquiry.

This time I raised my head from the thrilling cushion of her breast to stare at her.

Eyes, liquid and hypnotic, held mine. "Touch me," she said and watched as I ran my hand over the firm, flat plane of her belly past the fine trimmed hair at her groin until warm slippery film slathered my fingers. I slid back and forth, pressing down on her clit with the heel of my hand, teasing more wetness from between her rigid pink folds. I was so completely lost in sensation, I didn't even pause to wonder if I was using the right pressure or how long I should arouse her manually before switching from fingers to mouth.

After a while, Layla opened her thighs a little more and said, "Get inside."

I had never been so turned on in my life, and somewhere, lurking in the back of my mind, the knowledge that this was probably a big mistake and I should stop right now made the moment even more thrilling.

Hot, juicy flesh trapped my fingers as she drew me deep within. Walls of muscle seized hold and sucked. She pulled me down on her and bit into my shoulder just hard enough to jam every frequency with sensation. The smell of her, the slippery heat around my fingers, the taste of her mouth, the small implosion of pain and pleasure where her teeth were anchored, all combined to make me groan.

"You're so beautiful," I whispered in her ear between sharp breaths. "All wet and open and perfect."

She kissed me hard and her body rocked against mine. She slid a hand between my legs and made me crazy by stroking me slowly and relentlessly. I couldn't think. I was mesmerized by the slick play of fingers and flesh, that restless fluttering ensnarement, and my own helpless spiral toward ecstasy. Dimly aware of panting and moaning, and of her ragged little whispers getting more and more insistent, I curled my fingers up slightly and increased pressure against her pubic bone.

She responded by half-sobbing, "Oh, baby. Yeah. Come on." She continued to gasp out a steady litany of enticements. Her cheeks were stained red and her gaze was narcotic, eyes black with desire, heavy lids drooping.

Driven by her demands and my own frantic need to come and yet to make the pleasure last forever, I strained for release, sliding my clit back and forth along her hand, all the while fucking her harder. Sweat made us glide against one another, hot and shaking, heaving and thrusting.

I wanted to watch her come. I wanted to see everything fall away, leaving her true self naked with mine. Could she be any more beautiful than she was right now, with her back arched, her throat exposed, her breasts taut? I had to push her over the edge because I wanted to be there to catch her, to hold her and cherish her.

In my ear, she whispered, "It's okay. I'm right here with you."

I kissed the pulse that quivered at her neck and let myself merge with her and fly with her, lost in the crazy joy of our fuck. Exquisite tension climbed until I could bear it no longer. I pushed down hard on her hand, and in that moment, she crushed my fingers until I no longer knew where our flesh was divided. My mouth found hers and we melted into one another, sharing the same rippling shocks of release, the same sweet floating transcendence as our bodies spilled over, then relaxed.

Afterward, we lay perfectly still and I could feel her heart kneading mine. Afraid to move, yet afraid I was hurting her, I withdrew my hand a fraction. She whimpered and I froze, wondering what to do. I sensed in her a profound craving that had nothing to do with sex but was something else entirely.

"Tell me what you need," I said, kissing her hair.

"Can I sleep here?" She sounded small. Lost. Incredibly sad.

The need I could feel in her drowned out the tiny voice hammering away in the back of my mind. I didn't care if it was a bad idea. "Yes, please," I said.

Slowly, she eased her hand from between my legs. We rocked against one another, my fingers still snugly inside of her. She nuzzled into me, her head on my shoulder, her arm across me. Her contented little sighs were the same snuffling sounds that I was always too embarrassed to make, lying in the arms of my various sexual partners. By tiny degrees, I slid out of the hot cocoon of her body, then she held me tight and rolled me onto my side to face her. As naturally as if we'd done so a thousand times, we snuggled closer and lay in sated silence until our breathing grew deep and quiet.

She touched my cheek just as I was drifting off. "That was wonderful."

"Mmm-hmm." I thought if I spoke I might burst into tears.

She stared into my eyes. "Now, do you know you're a lesbian?"

I laughed and we fell asleep in one another's arms. Much later, I woke up and hazily pulled the quilt over us. Layla had shifted onto her side fetuslike, her knees drawn up, her arms crossed over her breasts. I curled drowsily against her and smiled. If home was meant to feel like heaven, this was home.

CHAPTER NINE

W hat on earth is going on here?" Mrs. Standish stood at the end of the bed, Eric at her side. Both wore expressions of incredulity.

I scrambled onto my butt, dragging some sheet up to cover my breasts. Next to me, Layla rolled over, blatantly naked and sleep tousled. She propped herself on her elbows and blinked at our early morning visitors. I waited for her to come up with the perfect, plausible answer that would defuse this explosive situation.

"I didn't mean to seduce her," she said, totally blowing it. "We were drunk and it just happened."

I gasped.

Like a man tormented, Eric clapped his hand to his forehead. "Oh, God. I trusted you alone with her and this is what you do?"

I stammered, "I'm sorry." But no one was listening to me.

"Layla, how could you?" Mrs. Standish said. "We've all made allowances for you over the years. But this?"

Eric wasn't finished. "You know exactly what I've been through— how hard this is for me. You know how I've struggled to find a woman I could adore. And you do...*this*! What were you thinking?"

Mrs. Standish gathered Eric into her arms, an elegant lioness in defense of her cub. Haughtily, she regarded us to one side of his quivering shoulder. "Please leave this house immediately," she told Layla. "I shall be speaking with your mother."

"Please don't, Aunt Patty. This was a terrible mistake." Layla inched her way farther up the bed and propped herself against the headboard, cursorily pulling a piece of sheet up. It covered almost nothing. "I take complete responsibility," she said. "Chance is not to blame."

Mrs. Standish's glacial blue eyes shifted to me. I wasn't sure what I read in them. Distaste. Anger. Pity. Condemnation. "You, my dear, are young and foolish," she pronounced. "I have no doubt you will repent your poor judgment at your leisure. But I have my family to think about. I must therefore ask you to leave as well."

Thank God. Relief at being able to escape made me relax a little, but my throat still hurt as if I were a genuine fiancée caught cheating on a genuine partner. The home-wrecker sitting next to me seemed to be trying to look embarrassed and shamefaced, yet at the same time she wore an air of brazen satisfaction that almost demanded a slap across the face. I wanted to shove her and say: *What's wrong with you? This is his mother!* I also wanted to kiss her, to elope with her to a distant isle where we could dine eternally on the fruits of love.

Eric stepped out of Mrs. Standish's maternal embrace, but took her beautifully manicured hand as if drawing on her strength. The epitome of grace under pressure, he said, "Yes, I think that would be best, Chance. I'm only thankful Dad didn't have to see this."

I thought: *And the Oscar for best actor goes to…* In that moment I could see exactly what he was up to. He was exploiting an opportunity. He knew I wanted out of this absurd farce, and so did he. Now, here was the perfect means. He wouldn't have to explain a thing, and his mother—who appeared to be truly in denial—would not blame him for any of this. Apparently, she had convinced herself that Eric was not completely gay, but a bisexual trying to steer his inclinations in the procreative direction for the sake of the family. I was a symbol of hope. Dispensable, because if Eric was willing to marry me that meant there would be another girl, another day. And probably one who would look prettier in a big dress.

I stole a sideways glance at Layla, marveling that she had been able to play along with this without missing a beat. As soon as I had that thought, another scenario presented itself. Had she and Eric cooked this up between them ahead of time? Was that why she didn't seem especially surprised by the arrival of her aunt and cousin just in time to catch us in bed together? It seemed too much of a coincidence that Eric had just stumbled into my bedroom with his mother first thing in the morning. He must have known what to expect.

My mouth seemed to fill with sand as this train of thought rattled irrevocably toward the only logical conclusion. They had planned cold-bloodedly for Layla to seduce me. I recalled our interaction two evenings earlier. I had known then that she could see right through me. Had she confronted Eric with her suspicions? Had he spilled everything, and had they then hatched a plan to end the fake engagement while making sure Eric's mother could still fool herself about his sexuality?

The more I thought about it, the more likely it seemed. Layla hadn't been overcome with desire for me. She hadn't set common sense aside because she was attracted to me as much as I was to her. She had simply used her power. Maybe the plan was her idea. She knew I would be a pushover, and Eric had probably assumed I was so smitten I'd be thrilled to sleep with her no matter how it came about.

I met his eyes and caught a flash of guilt and pleading that told me my imagination was not running away with me. Humiliated, I said, "Mrs. Standish, I owe you an apology. I was dishonest and behaved against my better judgment. I should not have come here."

It gave me some comfort to see Eric's eyes widen in panic and his shoulders tense as he waited to discover what else I was going to say.

Mrs. Standish was gracious. "I accept your apology, Chantelle. You're young and inexperienced, and you were affected by alcohol. I just hope this situation has taught you something and that you'll carry this lesson forward into the future. I truly wish you only the best."

She had never wanted me for a daughter-in-law; that much was obvious. I could see this magnanimous forgiveness didn't cost her too dearly.

"I've certainly learned my lesson," I said. "I'm going to take a shower and pack, then maybe someone could drive me to the airport."

Mrs. Standish said she'd speak to the gardener, but Layla announced, "I'll be driving to Los Angeles. I can take you that far, then you could catch a flight to San Francisco."

Eric shook his head. "That won't be necessary. Chance and I should talk."

"No kidding," I said.

He gave me a pleading look. "Take all the time you need. I'll wait downstairs."

He took Mrs. Standish's arm and without another word they swept from the room. In their wake, Layla and I sat in silence. She avoided my eyes.

"I'm sorry things turned out this way," she said eventually.

"Which way?" I decided not to make it easy for her.

She got out of bed and put on her robe. "I know you and Eric are very fond of one another. I hope this doesn't affect your friendship."

"I have a question for you," I said, still hoping I was wrong somehow and that she had not planned this ahead of time. "Did Eric know he was going to find you in my bed this morning?"

She took a few steps closer and said, "I owe you an explanation." I caught my breath at the pained candor I saw in her eyes. She seemed genuinely upset. "It's a very difficult situation. There's only so much I can tell you."

Whatever was going on in this mess of a family, she was hiding something or protecting someone. I had no idea what or who and I wasn't sure if I even cared. I just wanted to know if she had any feelings for me at all or if I had been used from the get-go, first by Eric, then by her.

"You can keep your secrets," I told her coldly, determined not to be suckered by this show of contrition. "I really don't care. But tell me one thing. Would you have wanted to sleep with me if you and Eric hadn't cooked up this little family drama for whatever bizarre reason you had?"

She pushed her hair back wearily, and I saw a faint reddish mark on her throat. I remembered my mouth lingering on that tiny, perfect inch of flesh and it all rushed back at me. Everything. The hot, wet, breathless, aching, noisy, urgent feast we'd shared. The cries and kisses. The longing finally assuaged. That same longing was present once more as I stared at her. Yet it was tinted with bitterness.

Evasively, she said, "I don't blame you for being angry. But can't we agree to just accept last night for what it was? We both had a good time. Do the hows and whys really matter?"

"You didn't answer my question."

Eventually she sighed a response to my stony remark. "Under normal circumstances, this probably wouldn't have happened. Okay?"

I forced my face muscles to stay very still. With dignity, I said, "Thank you."

She flinched. "Chance...please. I like you, and since we're telling the truth, last night was special. I'll always remember it."

I gave in to a cynical smile at this obvious attempt to soften the truth. "Yep. It's been...unforgettable. And now, if you don't mind, I have things to do."

"I guess this is good-bye." Her voice was husky and tinged with some emotion I could not identify. Regret? Even if that was what I saw, I knew I couldn't trust my eyes. For a split second her face seemed to beam an eloquent plea, then she was serene and Circe-like once more. "I wish you well, Chance."

I gave her a curt nod. "Bye, Layla."

She headed for the door and for a single, insane moment I contemplated running after her and dragging her back to bed so we could have sex again and prove there was something happening emotionally. Another fantasy promptly superseded this one: Layla turning around and rushing across the room to throw herself at me, telling me that she wanted us to be together without all the lies and games. That she felt something for me.

Of course, neither of these Hollywood endings happened, and as the door closed behind her, I felt something crumble inside. Dreams are fragile, and the siren who'd inhabited mine for so long had just tossed a grenade into the works. Nothing would be the same again.

CHAPTER TEN

Iused to carry around a four-leaf clover preserved in a block of plastic with *For Luck* emblazoned on it in gold. My father had brought it back from Ireland after a pilgrimage to his ancestral haunts. I imagined Irish families combing bogs for these rare symbols and selling them as keepsakes. Mom said it was more likely a whole village had built a cottage industry around gluing the extra leaf on millions of clovers.

Eventually I came to believe her, for far from stopping a bullet or ensuring a lottery win, my lucky clover ended up falling into a toilet bowl at a public bathroom along with my wallet. After the sordid rescue, I chiseled the token apart to discover once and for all whether it was a fraud. It was not, which proved that if a genuine good luck charm can end up in a toilet, we're in more trouble than we thought.

My life bore eloquent testimony to this. I left San Diego dogged with the awful suspicion that I would spend the rest of my days lamenting the loss of a woman I'd never really had in the first place. And I was soon to discover that the Fates had something even more disquieting in store for me.

It was late July and I was at Mrs. Goldman's, trimming between Quatro's toes, when Peaches stuck her head in the door and said, "Hey, babe. Can you sing?"

Assuming she was not talking to Mrs. Goldman, I replied with a firm shake of the head. "I'm tone deaf." I croaked a few bars of a Celine Dion song to demonstrate.

"Are you fucking crazy?" Peaches rushed in and clutched my arm. "You've got a voice like Patti Smith. You have *got* to try out for the band."

Their vocalist had gone to Seattle, she explained, to sing background for a bunch of jerks who'd just been signed by Geffen Records. How the fuck that had happened, she had no idea. Anyway, the suck-ass bitch wasn't coming back.

"Ever written a song?" she demanded.

"I can't even write my mom an e-mail."

"That's okay. You don't have to be a brain surgeon in this business." She tucked Hendrix under her arm. "We'll take the pooches. What the old lady doesn't know won't hurt her."

I picked up Quatro and followed Peaches downstairs. With every step I took, I felt the wheels of destiny turning. By the time we reached the basement, I had the giddy sensation that I had just leapt off a carousel and was about to jump onto a roller coaster. The other three women in the band greeted me with the kinds of dubious looks people give factory seconds.

"She's cool," Peaches insisted. Anxious to vindicate this claim, she ordered, "Sing something, babe."

A tall, lean woman with slicked back dark hair slowly chewed her gum as I vacillated. She stood slouched against a chair where a built-looking ash blonde in loose faded jeans and matte finish harness boots sat smoking a slender cigar, one leg slung over the chair arm. I'd seen her in the kitchen once or twice and she'd introduced herself as Lucrezia. Every time she looked at me my pulse hammered a nervous tattoo.

Peaches introduced the dark-haired woman as Siren, the drummer, and said Lucrezia played bass guitar and keyboard. All the while Lucrezia subjected me to an indolent appraisal that smacked of way too much self-assurance. This, I decided, was a woman who thought she could fuck anyone she wanted and probably expected them to be grateful. I was duly warned.

Peaches picked up her guitar and struck a few experimental chords as she waited for me to name a song. I didn't know any more than the chorus of most but, seized by an inspiration born of self-torture, I asked, "Can you play 'Layla'?"

Here was one song I knew inside out. I played it most nights as I sat in front of the computer composing letters Layla would never read, and checking Messenger every so often to see if Reverie was online. Her name hadn't lit up in the six weeks since the La Jolla debacle. I'd lost her too.

The band members stared at me like I was off another planet. "Clapton?" said the drummer.

"Yes," I replied unapologetically.

Peaches was already toying with the opening riffs. "Wanna cue me?" She reconsidered when I stared blankly at her. "Forget it. I'll count three, then you sing. Okay?"

It sounded so easy. Naturally I started on the wrong chord. Peaches adjusted to my wildly variant tempo like the song was meant to be played without any definite beat. I thought it sounded awful but Siren regarded me with a flicker of interest.

"Let's slow it down some." She sauntered over to her drums, picked up her drumsticks, and began tapping them rhythmically together.

Peaches played the opening riff, Siren worked up a compelling rhythm, and this time I hit the right chord and made it all the way to the chorus, somewhat embarrassed at the craving the song expressed. As we jammed, Lucrezia stubbed out her cigar and joined the disorderly session on keyboard. When I forgot the lyrics to the next verse, she sang with me. Not a great voice, but she knew every word of this yesteryear classic.

When we were done belting out the chorus one more time, Peaches stopped playing abruptly, and she and the others looked past me to a man who was standing just inside the door, his hands in the pockets of an impressively tailored suit. Hendrix and Quatro circled his legs, their tufted white tails wagging.

He strolled into the room, his expression speculative. "Smart move, dumping the chick with the bad skin," he informed Peaches. Extending a hand to me, he asked, "Have I seen you somewhere?"

The guy had tipped me a hundred last time we met because his mother said I treated her like a queen. "I'm the dog groomer," I reminded him.

"Of course. Chantelle, isn't it?"

"Yes, Mr. Goldman."

He grinned. His teeth were extraordinarily white. He wore a cream polo zipped at the neck and his wavy black hair looked like it had just been blow-dried into one of those male model styles. "Well, Chantelle. You just got yourself a new career."

Peaches looked flushed. "I finished those songs, Mr. Goldman."

"Okay. Good." He paced the concrete floor, then stopped dead. As though stupefied by his own genius, he flung both hands in the air and announced, "The Brits have Joss Stone, but we're packaging nitwit bimbos who can't sing. It's time for raw talent again. The planet is ready and the stocks are low. We've got Alanis. Annie Lennox is on a comeback. kd lang is still doing that gender-fuck thing. Madonna's got kids but she can fill a stadium. *And* there's Enya."

What was his point? Women could sell records? Clearly Peaches figured that's what he was getting at. Waving a hand in my direction, she said, "We can work on the look."

"What's your range?" he asked me.

"Canine Follies pays me fifteen bucks an hour."

He stared at me like I was mentally disabled, then he took Peaches's arm and led her toward the door, communicating something in a terse undertone. I don't know what he said, but after he'd gone, she turned to us, white-faced and palpitating.

"Fuck," she breathed. "He's signing us and we're all going to get paid."

"Are you serious?" Lucrezia looked me up and down like she knew how to get me wet.

Peaches emitted a happy little squeal and hugged me to her. "Yes. All of us. Chance included."

I could feel my face compressing into a bewildered squint. "But I can't sing."

Bella, the saxophonist, who had shown up just as Mr. Goldman left said, "You're a skinny white girl living in America. You think it matters if you can't sing?"

❖

That was how I stumbled into the music business. No training. No musical talent. Everything Mrs. Goldman despised.

When she heard I might have to take time out from grooming Hendrix and Quatro, she said, "I knew you were a singer."

"Your son is going to record us," I replied.

"Don't get started on drugs. The only thing you want up your nose is fresh air."

"I'm staying on with Canine Follies," I assured her. "You'll have a temporary groomer then I'll be back."

"You gonna change your name? Most singers change their name."

"I'm sticking with Chance. Your son likes it."

Mr. Goldman said it had "legend potential." Like everything else he said, it sounded too good to be true.

"Hire a good attorney," Mrs. Goldman advised, feeding Godiva chocolates to Hendrix, "or my son will keep all your money."

She sounded so matter-of-fact in this harsh opinion, I felt I should defend the man who might pluck me from obscurity. "Mr. Goldman has been very supportive," I said.

"Read the small print," she replied, unimpressed.

❖

I shared Mrs. Goldman's advice with the rest of the band, who seemed unconcerned. Virgin Blessing, I learned, had been around for several years, mostly playing covers at small venues. I had probably heard them at a women's event some time and forgotten.

After hearing a demo tape, Samuel Goldman had offered them his mother's basement and told them to write some original material and get a sound that was different from Bananarama. The rest was history, or it would be by the time we were interviewed in *Rolling Stone*.

"He loves you," Peaches said. "He says you're a mixture of Billie Holiday and Janis."

"Does he know I'm a dyke?"

"I told him you were vegetarian," she said, like the two were synonymous.

We were in Mrs. Goldman's basement rehearsing the new songs Peaches had written over the past couple of months since I'd joined the band. Mr. Goldman was coming to hear us shortly. We had done the work on my look that Peaches thought was important. My hair was dyed platinum blonde, with hints of pink showing through where the chemicals had burnt my scalp. I wore pale foundation, dark eye make-up, and lipstick that made my mouth look like red plastic. Worse still, I was supposed to strut around in a skintight pink latex top, black pants with graffiti all over them, and red patent leather Doc Marten boots.

My fellow band members whistled when Peaches dragged me out of the bathroom.

Siren said, "You'll make everyone happy, the girls and the boys."

Bella took a moment out from polishing her sax. A woman of few words from a family of many jazz musicians, she said, "Okay."

Easy for her, I thought. She had so much talent she didn't have to doll herself up to get attention. Even more unfairly, she had the born-beautiful good looks so many African American women could take for granted. Her teeth were white and perfect, her skin was a gorgeous shade of sugar brown, and her dark hair was naturally curly and always braided and beaded immaculately. I thought she must have a proud mother who endlessly groomed her, but actually, she had a sister who owned a beauty shop.

We all had our hair done there. DeVonna, the sister, had tried to talk me out of the platinum blonde into sleek black hair like Siren's, but Peaches insisted. No one else in the band had hair like mine and dyed and spiky, even the tuft behaved itself.

Lucrezia, who looked sublimely comfortable as usual, in black jeans and a muscle T-shirt, added her husky approval to everyone else's. "Yeah. It works."

Peaches tuned her guitar and played a riff from one of the songs I'd been learning.

I said, gloomily, "I still can't remember how it goes."

"You're doing fine." As usual, Lucrezia's steady gaze reminded me that I was pathetically horny. "How are the lessons going?"

"Good."

Mr. Goldman was paying big bucks for a famous voice coach for me. Four times a week, we spent two hours together in Maestro Julio's studio, him on the piano, me singing la-la-la-la—la-la-la-la—*lah* over and over until I knew the difference between G and C, and could sing a flat and a sharp note on command. Instead of liver treats when I performed these tricks, I got to take a moment and gargle. Between times, we did breathing exercises in yoga positions and the Maestro would stick his hand between my shoulder blades and talk about vibration and the natural harmony of body and soul. I thought he should meet my parents. He was right up their street.

"I can hear the difference," Lucrezia said. "There's more control and your range is better by about five notes."

"Thanks." This was the most our hunky bass guitarist had ever said to me.

Lucrezia sang backup, along with Peaches. When my voice was working better, Mr. Goldman said the three of us would have lessons together to work on our harmonies. In this business, you needed to make the most of raw talent if you had any. "Look what Madonna achieved with a very average set of vocal cords," he would tell us.

I leafed through the handwritten sheet music until I located the track Peaches thought would be our first single. I was supposed to snarl my way through the suggestive lyrics, which was a blessing because I could not make rapid chromatic changes and stay in tune at the same time. But I was giving it my best shot when Mr. Goldman arrived with a dark-haired woman wearing groovy little half-moon glasses with crimson plastic frames. I recognized her instantly and my snarl became a whimper. Layla.

They approached. She stared at me. I stopped singing and the band lapsed into silence.

Mr. Goldman said, "This is Layla Wilde. She writes hit songs for Goldman Music, and she's worked up a couple of singles I want Virgin Blessing to record."

I sensed Peaches stiffen and caught something tense and aggravated in the way Lucrezia stared at Layla. It was unusual for her to react strongly to anyone, and almost as soon as I noticed the expression, she lowered her head and started tuning her guitar.

Layla barely glanced at her, saying to Peaches, "It's a real honor to meet you. I've heard some of your work. I like the way you blend punk and blues, especially on that track—" She began humming.

"'You Can't Run,'" Peaches identified the tune. "You heard the demo tape, huh?"

Layla nodded. "It's hot." She offered Peaches the pages she was holding. "Mr. Goldman asked me to come up with a rock/pop crossover with some punk edge and a great vocal hook for your new lead." She stared pointedly at me as Peaches and the other band members huddled together and studied the music. "How's it going, Chance?"

"Excellent," I said, miserably conscious of my glam appearance.

"You didn't tell me you were a musician."

"I'm not."

She subjected me to a single raised eyebrow. "Good impersonation."

I blushed and became aware of an assessing look from Lucrezia.

"What are you doing later?" Layla asked, ignoring the glances my companions were casting in our direction.

"Rehearsing," I said.

"Maybe you can wrap it up early. You and I should spend some time together so we can discuss a few ideas I have. I need to know more about your vocal qualities."

Lucrezia choked and wandered over to the piano, where she started tinkering with a few melody lines.

Ignoring her, and apparently taking my stymied silence for assent, Layla nudged her little glasses back into place. "What say I pick you up here at nine?"

Feeling sick to my stomach, I said, "If you think it's necessary."

She gave me a cool smile. "I'll look forward to it."

I shrugged and signaled Peaches that I was ready to continue. Lucrezia played the opening bars of a familiar tune and this time anger flickered across Layla's expression. I recognized "The Bitch Is Back" and stared across at Lucrezia, bemused. Was this ungallant theme a random choice, or was she being protective of Peaches and expressing her displeasure about a name songwriter being brought in? She certainly seemed unimpressed with Layla, which surprised me because Layla was exactly the kind of dark-haired beauty Lucrezia usually took home after gigs.

"Okay, let's do this." Mr. Goldman interrupted his cell phone call to signal that we should get to work. He exchanged a few words with Layla and she gave us a casual wave and strolled away, apparently untroubled.

I was worried about contributing to the kind of music I hated—loud and raw with no discernable lyrics, or lyrics so moronic it's a good thing they're drowned out by the guitars. But noise terrorism was not Layla's style. The songs she'd written for us had Grammy nomination stamped all over them. I could see why Mr. Goldman was shifting in his seat as Peaches began picking out the melody lines. The scent of money makes music industry people itchy.

"I can't reach these notes," I said, as Peaches played the chorus.

She switched immediately to a different chord. "How 'bout that?"

Lucrezia picked up the bass, filling out the sound. I experimented with a few bars. Even this stumbling first attempt sounded promising. The melody gave me time to breathe and I found I was suddenly singing more freely. Lucrezia was right. The Maestro was paying off.

"Well, it's different," Siren said, when we'd gotten through the first verse and chorus.

Mr. Goldman fished some papers out of his briefcase and came over. "This is your recording contract. Read it and sign it. Oh yeah, and think up a name for your album. I want you ready to lay down the first tracks next month."

I could feel my jaw slipping as it dawned on me that this was for real. I could no longer play at being a singer, I would have to work.

Mr. Goldman draped an arm over my shoulder and flashed his snazzy white dental art. "You gals," he decreed, "are in for one helluva ride."

❖

"Are you sure you want to hang around?" Lucrezia asked.

She was the last to leave. It was slightly after nine and I expected Layla would walk in the door at any moment. I had no idea how I felt about that. Excited. Angry. Hot.

"She'll show up," I said. "And Mr. Goldman won't be happy if I stand her up."

Lucrezia fastened her guitar case and pulled on an old biker jacket. "You have a great voice," she surprised me by saying. "I'm glad you joined the band."

"Thanks. Me too."

Her sleepy greenish hazel eyes moved slowly over my body and finally rested on my face. "Give me your cell and I'll put my number on your speed dial. That way, if you're ever at a loose end and you want to go out for a drink, you can call me."

I handed over my cell phone, somewhat disconcerted by this offer. Was Lucrezia hitting on me?

Reading my mind, she said nonchalantly, "Sometimes it's good to socialize with another band member. We all know where we stand with each other."

I watched her key in the numbers and felt a familiar flutter in the pit of my stomach. Instantly, I wanted to slap some sense into myself. Lucrezia was offering to be my buddy, and here I was speculating on how it might be to get naked with her. She handed me the phone and I thanked her, trying to sound natural.

"Catch you later," she said.

"Yeah, tomorrow at five, right?"

"Right." She gave me one of her rare wolfish smiles and stalked away, her guitar slung over one shoulder.

Yet again I lapsed into fantasy. It was hard not to. Lucrezia was one of those women who oozed sex. You only had to look at her and you knew she was an accomplished lover. She was the reason women hung around our rehearsals and bought us drinks after gigs. Peaches was always teasing her about this woman or that. It sounded like she had more sexual partners than she could count.

Out in the real world, she was a home renovation contractor with a few guys working for her. The outdoor job accounted for her tan, the bleached streaks in her ash blonde hair, and her muscles. Lucrezia was always inspecting her hands and rubbing cream into them. She took her guitar playing very seriously and needed not to have calluses in the wrong places. This was what Peaches told me after I once made a comment about these preparatory rituals.

I looked up her number in my cell phone, and my breathing got short and stifled. I could still feel her unsettling stare. How would it be having her for a friend, if that's all she was looking for? A vague disappointment snapped at my throat, corroding my sense of gratification. I respected Lucrezia. She and Bella were the two band members who really had their shit together. I felt honored that she wanted to be my friend, yet at the same time I felt a bothersome prick of rejection.

It was ridiculous, of course. I wasn't her type and even if I were, having a fling with a band member would be a crazy idea. Besides, I was besotted with another woman. Turning my thoughts to Layla, I wandered around the basement, switching off most of the bright lights. When the place looked as ambient as I could make it, I settled down on one of the sofas we'd arranged into a living area. The furniture was a mismatched collection of Mrs. Goldman's discards. We had a leather chaise lounge with piping the Maltese terriers had chewed the crap out of, a huge feather-stuffed cream pullout Siren slept on when she was having fights with her boyfriend, worn-out armchairs in floral tapestry and velvet, and a saggy corduroy love seat with arms big enough to sit on.

I was sprawled on this with my legs propped on one of the arms when the door opened at the far end of the room and brilliant light shone in from the hallway that led outside.

Layla stood there for a moment, her perfect shape dramatically backlit, then she called, "Chance?"

"Over here." I hauled myself into a sitting position.

"Sorry I'm late. I was in a meeting with Samuel." Car keys jangled in her hand, knocking against the satchel she was carrying. She was wearing fashionable pin-striped pants and a crisp white shirt fitted to show off her curves. She looked so desirable I was instantly aware of needing a shower and being in the scruffy jeans and T-shirt I'd changed back into after Mr. Goldman left.

"Have you eaten?" she asked.

"We ordered pizza earlier."

She perched on an arm of the love seat and regarded me seriously. "You look good."

"You too." Polite and noncommittal.

"Still angry with me?"

"No," I said coolly. "That was then. This is now. Look, it's getting kind of late for me to be finishing work. What did you want to talk about?"

She hesitated as if she wanted to say something else, then opened her satchel and drew out a sheaf of papers. I found myself mesmerized by her hands. The long slender fingers, the latticework of veins beneath the fine skin, the fluid way the muscles worked, making her knuckles rise and whiten. I remembered those hands painting my skin with feeling.

She made a comment about my singing style. Lost, I asked, "Sorry, what was that again?"

"I said you have a bluesy grittiness in the low notes that I'd like to exploit."

"Knock yourself out. If I can't manage your melody line, Peaches will change the key."

"No, she won't. Not for this song." Layla handed me some sheet music. "Samuel tells me Julio is working with you. I'm going to come along to your next lesson and let him know exactly what I want."

"You're what?"

"I said—"

"I heard you the first time." Okay. I was getting angry and it showed. I didn't want Layla showing up at my singing lessons. I didn't want her invading my life in any way that wasn't necessitated by a direct order from my new boss.

"Chance, I'm here to help," she said. "Your band has a unique sound. You could break through, but it's not easy for women. Actually, it's not easy for anyone. This business stinks. It's too much about marketing these days, and less about talent."

"We're not doing this because we want to be famous," I said nobly. "We like playing. If we could make a living at it, that would be great, but if we can't it's still fun."

"You don't have to settle for that," she said. "You have a fantastic voice."

I laughed. "I can hardly remember the lyrics. I can't sing a note unless I spend hours practicing it with Maestro Julio. Somehow I don't think I'm naturally gifted."

She gave me an odd look and I stared down at the music I was holding. "What do you want me to do? Sing some of this?"

"No. I want to discuss the songs with you so that you understand what Mr. Goldman wants to hear." She sounded frustrated.

"Okay." I made room for her on the sofa. "You have my full attention. Tell me what Mr. Goldman wants."

She sat down next to me. She smelled musky sweet like Stargazer lilies. I wanted to bite her, but I took a notebook and pen from my backpack instead.

She touched my arm, which made me lose my concentration and drop everything. "Relax," she said. "So, what's happening in your life?"

"Other than joining the band, not much."

"Girlfriend?"

"One or two." Suck on that. For good measure, I informed her, "When you're in a band, they can't leave you alone."

"That must be fun," she said dryly.

I wanted to avoid staring at her mouth because it only made me want to kiss her, but I couldn't help noticing the way it creased in each corner as if she'd just suppressed a smile. "Women have always thrown themselves at me," I said, trying to sound cynically amused. "Take you, for example."

"Touché."

Knowing my little barb found its mark should have been gratifying, but I felt like I'd just slid into high school tit for tat. I wanted to let Layla know that I wasn't pining for her, by any means. I had no trouble getting laid, thank you very much. These days, I could walk into any lesbian venue and pick and choose. Women came up to *me*. Being in the band and being more proactive about my life was making me more confident, and confidence was attractive.

I supposed it also helped that my new look was cool. I had more style. When I stepped into a room, the conversation lulled for a few seconds. I'd never made heads turn in my life. Now, all of a sudden, I was aware of eyes on me and hands brushing my skin when women moved past. At first, I thought I was just imagining it. Now, I took it for granted. Things had changed for the better. My strategy was finally paying off.

Suzie said being in a band meant major sex appeal, but since Virgin Blessing wasn't exactly well known, I thought she was overestimating that factor. I had achieved what I'd set out to do the day I donated my TV to a worthy cause. I had reinvented myself, and the new Chance was much more interesting. She found panties that didn't belong to her down the back of her sofa and got flirtatious e-mails from women she'd only spoken to in passing. She found phone numbers in the back pockets of her jeans and had no idea where they came from. She was hot.

I knew Layla had noticed the change in me. Her eyes patrolled my body with undisguised sexual interest. If I played my cards right, I could sleep with her again. That's if I wanted to, which I did not. At least intellectually; my body had its own agenda. But I could exercise control over that. I wasn't desperate anymore. I could leave here and phone Lucrezia. We could hit a club. I wouldn't be going home alone.

In what I hoped was a sophisticated drawl, I asked Layla, "How about you? Sucking the marrow from life?"

"More like choking on the bones." Her mouth relaxed into a half-smile, the lips invitingly parted. "My mom was livid over what happened in La Jolla. It made the funeral rather awkward."

What did she want from me? Sympathy? I said, "I'm sure she'll get over it."

She stared at me. "I can see you're going to make this hard."

I conceded this with a careless shrug. "Perhaps we should stick to talking shop. Isn't that why you're here?"

She sighed. "Okay, let's discuss how you're going to make your audience eat out of your hand."

"I'd like to see that."

"You will," she stated with conviction. "In fact, I bet you five thousand bucks and a one-night stand that today in a year's time, you'll have a hit album and your face on the cover of *Rolling Stone*."

Of course, just as she'd intended, all I really heard was "one-night stand." I said, "If you want to throw your money and your body away, who am I to object?"

She held my gaze. "Pretending to be hard doesn't suit you."

I willed the muscles in my face not to move. Layla was reacting to my cynical, who-cares? attitude. I was gratified. Two could play at her game. I replied, "Pretending to be soft doesn't suit you."

This time she looked away first and her chest rose and fell unevenly. "Let's get to work," she said thinly.

And that's what we did. It was almost midnight by the time she'd taught me how to sing her songs so I hit every emotional chord she'd written into them. I had no idea how badly I'd been interpreting them until she showed me where I needed to breathe and pause and slow my delivery down, which words to grind out and which to linger over like a slow tender kiss.

"You write really passionate songs," I said when we were through.

I was almost ashamed of myself for my flippant attitude earlier. Obviously Layla felt things deeply but seldom let others into her private world. Tonight she had invited me in and now that it was time to say good-bye, I was reluctant to leave.

"I guess I do," she said, putting her notes away in her satchel.

I stood at the same time she did. Impulsively, I asked, "Want to get a drink somewhere?"

She paused and her eloquent bruised violet eyes sought mine. "Let's avoid complication."

I pulled on my jacket and swung my backpack over my shoulder. "How complicated is a vodka and lime?"

"How complicated do you want it to be?" Her smile was tempered by a caustic sadness.

I said, "I really appreciate what we did here tonight, Layla, and I'm sorry if I was a jerk at first. I'd like to buy you a drink. That's all."

She stepped toward me and slid the palm of her hand up my cheek until her fingers were buried in my hair. Feeling her so close made my legs weak and my head spin. In the thrall of her enchantment, I was aware of rational thought processes shutting down and my common sense exiting stage right. My cheek was hot where she held it. My throat was tight, and my eyes wanted to slide shut in anticipation of a kiss. But uncertainty kept me staring at her, trying to decipher her intentions.

She brushed her lips so lightly across mine I could have mistaken breath for skin. "I wish things were different," she said so quietly the words were hard to make out. "I wish I could turn back time. Maybe I'd have something to offer you."

I stayed frozen, trembling on the brink of kissing her back. I hardly dared believe the softness in her face, the wistful longing in her gaze. My body clamored, every fiber fully charged and tingling. My spine was rigid as if transferring voltage to every nerve. I couldn't resist. I let my backpack slide to the floor and lifted my index finger to the hollow at the base of her throat, stroking the delicate ridge of bone. Through my fingertip, I felt her swallow. She drew a sharp breath and angled her head very slightly, inviting my kiss.

"I want you, Layla," I said weakly.

"I'm not a groupie."

"Thank God for that." I allowed my hand to drift to the back of her neck. Fine wisps of hair wrapped around my fingers. "Where are you staying?"

"What are you asking?"

The voice of reason instantly boomed from the back of my mind, pointing out that the last time Layla slept with me she'd had an agenda. I'd hoped there was more to it than that, but she did not even bother to contact me after I left San Diego. A woman who was really interested in me would have phoned. She knew how to get hold of me. All she had to do was ask Eric for my number. But she hadn't.

Worse still, when I finally called the number Eric had given me on our awkward drive to San Diego airport, all I got was an answering machine. Layla called me back only after I left several messages. She was in the Czech Republic and had no plans to return for some time. In a carefully worded brush-off, she'd made it clear we were 100% history and what had happened between us was nothing more than a lapse in judgment on her part and wish fulfillment on mine.

I wasn't so desperate that I had to settle for that kind of treatment from anyone, let alone a woman I could easily fall in love with and almost had. Did I really want to invite certain heartbreak into my life?

I took a determined step back, easing myself from her embrace, instantly missing the heat where our bodies had connected. My thoughts were scrambled. Maybe it *wouldn't* be heartbreak. Maybe we could just have some fun. Yet if I did what my body wanted, I had a bad feeling about the consequences. I scrutinized her face seeking clues to her true feelings.

She returned my stare with the same disarming candor that had made me lower my guard in San Diego. "Chance?"

Knowing I was being a fool, but unable to help myself, I said, "It was good the first time. So, I thought maybe we could hook up again. No strings."

"You have a point." She seemed to consider this suggestion seriously. "We're two consenting adults. We're allowed to have sex just because we feel like it."

"Exactly."

Her expression remained pensive. "I like you, Chance. And you're a good sexual partner."

"Gee, thanks. That's a relief."

My sour note didn't appear to register. "It's not like we're declaring undying love," she mused. "We don't have to commit to anything."

I had the discouraging impression that she was trying to persuade herself. Her clinical detachment made one thing very obvious—she had no feelings for me. I could be anyone. We were not discussing a possible future as lovers, we were coming to an agreement about the terms of a sexual encounter. This time no one was laboring under any delusions.

"Yep. Easy come, easy go." I tried to keep my voice playful. The last thing I wanted was for her to know how irrationally hurt I was. No other woman had ever gotten under my skin the way she had. I was angry with myself that she still had the power to disturb me.

"You sound bitter," she said, seemingly at a loss. "If you can't let go of the past, there's no way we can have something casual now."

"If I can't let go maybe that's because I have hurt feelings." I didn't want to get into a heavy conversation, but the words just spilled out. "You've never even said you're sorry."

"You want an apology from me?"

"That would be nice."

She gave me a strange, fierce look. "Let me see. We were both horny. We were both laboring under delusions. We both wanted what happened. We both had a good time. But *I* should apologize?"

Infuriated, I said, "You left something out. *You* had an agenda that I knew nothing about. Do you think I'd have slept with you if I did?"

"In a word, yes."

Her arrogance knew no bounds. I threw up my hands in disbelief. What was wrong with the woman? "You're a piece of work."

"Oh, grow up," she threw at me. "I thought I was doing you a favor."

"Fuck you," I said.

Which made her even madder. I was intrigued to see her usual serenity eclipsed by a riot of emotions. Her cheeks glowed bright red and her eyes flashed cold rage at me. "Your recollection of events is somewhat selective," she said icily. "I thought you were trying to prove you could be straight by marrying Eric. I felt sorry for you. I wanted to help you accept who you really were."

"Oh, I see. So you're off the hook. It was my fault we ended up sleeping together."

She let out an impatient sigh. "I know you don't want to hear it, but the truth is we conned each other. You let me believe the poor-confused-coming-out bullshit, and I didn't tell you I had a deal with Eric to be in your bed the next morning. But we were good together." Her eyes pleaded with me. "There was nothing phony about that part."

"Whatever." I wanted to believe her, but the truth was, I didn't trust her. It was that simple. Filled with misery, I picked up my backpack once more, signaling an end to our discussion.

For some reason this made her lose her temper all over again. "Chance, you're being completely unreasonable. I'm not denying it was fucked up. All I know is Eric came out of that mess with exactly what he wanted, and you and I ended up having *this* conversation instead of fucking our brains out at my hotel."

I wavered, stuck on her final comment and captivated by the passionate woman her anger revealed. Shame crept up on me. There *were* two sides to what had happened; I knew that in my heart. I had avoided taking responsibility for my part in that seduction because it was easier to blame her. Being angry at Layla took my mind off my darker thoughts—that she was the woman of my dreams and she had been served up by the Fates but I had somehow failed to claim her. I feared my ineptitude would haunt me forever.

Wondering how I could end this without making matters any worse than they were, I said, "I'm sorry for shouting at you."

Her face softened. "I'm sorry too. I never meant to hurt you."

"Thanks," I mumbled.

"I think it would be a mistake for us to get personally involved... on any level," she said. "You see that, don't you?"

"Yeah, who needs the drama?" Even if we could both agree to forgive and forget, it was probably a bad idea to start seeing each other, and I would be kidding myself if I thought I could settle for a fling. Wanting to let her know that I could be adult about this, I said, "I'm really glad we could work on the songs together. I think it'll make a big difference."

"Chance..." she chided softly and closed the distance between us. Looking me in the eye, she said, "You're a smart, talented, sweet woman and one day you'll meet someone wonderful. That's what you deserve."

"I just want to know one thing," I responded. "Why can't that woman be you? Am I not your type, or what?"

Her eyes welled. "It's nothing to do with you. I can't be in a relationship right now, that's all. Maybe one day that will change, but in the meantime..."

I thought back to the night we'd gone swimming and wondered what it was she'd been on the brink of telling me when she showed me the scars of her stabbing. The same unguarded mix of hope and doubt was on her face now. I could almost see her misgivings smothering the urge to reach out.

Recklessly, I grabbed her hand. "Layla, what is it? Please tell me."

She looked touched, and so desolate I yearned to make things right for her. "I don't want to start down that track," she said. "It's late, and we're done here. Go home and get some sleep. Let's just put all this behind us and focus on getting that Grammy nomination."

I could see her closing herself down as she spoke, getting distance from whatever menace lay coiled behind the mental door she refused to open. People with unbearable secrets had to cope any way they could.

If that's what she was harboring, I had no choice but to respect her wishes.

"Come on," I said. "I'll walk you to your car."

We turned out the lights, locked the doors, and made sure Mrs. Goldman's alarm system was fully activated. As we walked to the car, I switched to a safe topic.

"What are you writing at the moment?"

"A ballad." Her self-mockery was unmistakable. "The usual poor-me crap about wanting what you can't have."

She smiled her most alluring smile. Layla the temptress was once more calling the shots and needed to let me know her moment of weakness had passed. I was about to ask what it was that she wanted but couldn't have, when she wrapped a hand around the back of my neck and dropped a firm farewell kiss on my mouth.

CHAPTER ELEVEN

My parents looked stoned when I told them the happy news about my career change.

"We're proud of you, honey." Dad surveyed the rows of CDs lined up next to the stereo and gave a loud whistle. "I'll be damned—our own Barbra Streisand."

"Actually, there are five of us. We're a rock band. Kind of punk, really. We're called, er…" *Tell them*, I ordered myself.

"What do you mean?" Mom asked, marveling at my suicide blonde hair. "I hope you're not going to be playing heavy metal."

My father shook his head. "Women don't play that stuff. Far too smart. How about singing something for us, darling?"

I declined automatically, but their eager faces touched me. I could almost hear them boasting to friends and relatives: *Yes, she drives around in a limousine now.* They would never have to deal with another put-down over my lesbianism. They could look people in the eye and say: *Our daughter is famous, how about your kids?*

Mom served slices of turkey breast onto my plate. I had forgotten to tell her I was trying to be a vegetarian again and she'd made my favorite comfort food. It seemed churlish to decline, so I piled on the sweet potatoes and smothered everything in gravy.

"Promise me something, darling." Mom passed the cranberry sauce around. "Don't get involved with drugs. Look what happened to Janis Joplin. And there's Karen Carpenter and Mama Cass. Don't get an eating disorder. You don't have any weight to spare and you're beautiful just the way you are."

"Don't worry. I'll be fine." I had more pressing matters on my mind, like how I was going to sing in public without the words in front of me. Mr. Goldman was already talking about our first "serious" gig.

"Your life is going to be very different, now," Mom continued. "You'll be mixing with shallow, egotistical show-business people. It's only natural you'll want to fit in."

There was no point arguing. "Sure Mom. I'll watch out for weed and I won't skip meals."

"How much are they paying you?" Dad asked.

"I don't know, exactly. The accountants and lawyers are working on it."

He said, "A little more of that dark meat, thanks, Carol," then, to me, "You know, I never had you figured for a singer. Just goes to show. What'd you say your group was called?"

I chewed very slowly. I had prepared myself for this and the evil hour was upon me. "Blessing," I said. "Um…Virgin Blessing."

"Virgin's Blessing?" My mom.

"Virgin," I corrected. "Just plain Virgin."

"Mmm." She looked at my father.

Dad said, "What kind of a name is that?"

"Lots of singers are influenced by religion," I told him.

"Like Black Sabbath, for example?" He lowered his knife and fork. I could see the Irish Catholic chromosome making him twitchy.

"I'm not sure what the Holy Father would say," Mom worried. She could hang out with gurus and mumble Hare Krishna type chants up to a point, but for the big stuff she still called upon St. Jude and the BVM, which, for those of you unfamiliar with things Catholic, means Blessed Virgin Mary.

"Who's going to tell him?" I said.

"That's not the point." Dad resumed eating. "The point is, you could offend a lot of people with a name like that. Not everyone is as liberal minded as your mother and me."

I nodded solemnly. "It wasn't my idea. I wanted to call us…um…" I gazed down at my turkey, seeking inspiration. "The Cranberries. But there's a band with that name already."

"Virgin Blessing," Mom repeated. I could tell she was searching for a positive angle. "It makes an impression. People will remember it."

"We mean it respectfully," I said. "Two of the others are Catholics."

"Your mother and I saw the Rolling Stones live," Dad said. "Now that was a concert."

Mom sighed. "There's not much original music now, is there? Do you think MTV is the problem? Is the DVD more important than the music these days?"

Dad said, "There was plenty of junk around when we were kids, Carol. But we only remember the good stuff."

"I knew it was all over the day John Lennon was murdered." Mom headed for a safe and familiar track. "There's something terribly wrong with a society that murders its artists."

She often got emotional about the state of the world. It struck me that she and Reverie would have gotten along okay.

"No one's going to shoot me, Mom," I assured her, wishing as I so often did these days that Reverie wasn't lost to me. Countless Fridays had passed and she had not showed. I had e-mailed my pic to her and, in reply, received a resounding silence.

Mom patted my hand, her eyes distant. "Just remember what's important in life. You have to look at yourself in the mirror each morning."

Here it was, the perfect opening, the right time to bring up what I really wanted to discuss with my parents. Cautiously, I said, "While we're on that subject, can I talk with you guys about something?"

They gave me their undivided attention, and I almost decided, confronted with their tenderness, that I should just thank God for their unconditional love and forget what had increasingly preyed on my mind since San Diego. I should eat my roast turkey and kiss them farewell, and leave them at peace. I didn't have to do this to the people who had given me so much.

As I was vacillating, Mom touched my hand, "It's okay. I knew this day would come."

I looked up, startled and guilty. She had always seen right through me.

Confirming her maternal omniscience, she said, "It would be strange if you didn't want to know who she is."

At this point my father, completely lost, as usual, asked, "Who?"

I said with great difficulty, "The woman who gave birth to me."

Dad made an odd, winded sound and I could tell from the motion of his shoulder that his hand sought Mom's beneath the table. Instantly I wanted to tell them to forget I'd uttered a word.

"Please don't feel bad," I said, blinking away tears. "This isn't about you. You're my parents and nothing can change that. I love you both more than anything."

"We know," Mom said. "Your father and I have talked about this, obviously. And we'll help in any way we can."

My panic receded and I slowly exhaled. They were being so cool I didn't need to get hysterical. I had amazing parents. "Do you know her name?" I asked.

Mom shook her head. "We weren't allowed to know. It was a closed adoption. All I can tell you is what we were told."

"Which is that I was born in California to an unmarried mother," I repeated the one piece of information I'd been given for as long as I could remember.

Something tightened Mom's face. "There was one other thing." She exchanged a look with my dad. "We decided we wouldn't tell you until you asked."

She seemed upset and I got up and went to her, draping my arms around her neck. "We don't have to talk about it anymore. Okay?" I was unwilling to continue if it meant hurting her.

She kissed my cheek and I smooched against her soft, frizzy brown hair. "I'm not upset for myself, darling," she said. "It's just that it's always been difficult to know this…information, and not share it with you. We never wanted to conceal anything. But when you were younger…" She looked at Dad again.

"We thought it was the best thing for you," he said in a gravelly voice. He was upset too.

I had made both my parents cry. Terrific. Wonderful.

Mom shifted in her chair, took hold of my shoulders, and faced me squarely. As grave as I'd ever heard her, she said, "My beloved, your birth mother is incarcerated. She's serving a life sentence. I wish there was some other way to say this. You were born in prison."

❖

"So how was it?" Suzie asked.

We were in her courtyard, overdosing on pretzels, Buds, and seedy revelations about exes.

I hardly knew where to start. I was still shell shocked. "They're cool about the band," I said lamely.

"I love your parents. I wish they'd adopted me too."

"Can I run something by you?" I asked.

Suzie's eyes lit up. "You've met someone?"

"No, I've decided to trace my birth mother." I pondered on how much I was going to say. I didn't want to tell anyone about my place of birth, at least not until I could be absolutely certain that my mom hadn't got it wrong. I knew Suzie wouldn't get weird on me, but it didn't matter how nice she was about it, I was the offspring of a convicted felon. I felt humiliated.

Suzie held a pretzel poised. I put myself in her shoes for a moment. She'd known me for ten years. In that time, I had never once shown ambivalence about being adopted.

Looking like she was thinking carefully about her words, she said, "How do you go about it? I thought they sealed adoption records."

"They do, but there's an organization that puts mothers and their adopted children in touch. I know a couple of facts, so I phoned them and they told me the name of a good private investigator."

"Have you told your parents? I mean, most adopted kids are curious about their real mothers. Maybe they have some information."

Real mother. What a loaded phrase that was. "I look upon Mom as my real mother, Suzie."

She groaned. "I put my foot in it already."

I offered her the pretzels. "I'm being oversensitive. I told them over lunch yesterday and they're helping. Next week we have an appointment with a lawyer and the investigator."

"Wow." Suzie's expression was serious. "What are you going to do when you find her?"

"I'm not sure. I thought I'd write a letter first." Somehow I couldn't see myself showing up at a prison to visit a woman who had no idea who I was. That was not the best way to announce myself as the daughter she gave up twenty-seven years ago. I wondered what she'd done to deserve life imprisonment. It had to be murder. Did that make me a bad seed?

All of a sudden, I needed a hug, and I needed it from my mom, but I would have to settle for Suzie. I conjured up a vision of sitting on Mom's knee, inhaling the powdery scent of her, my ear pressed to the hollow between her breasts where her heart beat. Although she was resolute in her support of me as her gay daughter, she had withdrawn from me since I came out to her and we no longer shared the easy physical affection I'd known all through childhood.

I'd tried to convince myself this was perfectly natural, part of the inevitable transition from child to adult. But despite the rationalizations, I still felt hurt and rejected. I could not believe my gayness had made a difference. I wanted to think it was something else. I felt guilty and ashamed that I, so truly loved and wanted by my adoptive parents, could harbor this cargo of doubt and self-pity.

When I was with them, I concealed my traitorous emotions, keeping up a cheerful imitation of the daughter I'd always been. But I mourned constantly for the loss of that intimacy, for my mom's warm hand on my back and her constant kisses and pats. There's a reassurance and sense of belonging you can only get from the woman who nurtured you from helpless infancy to adulthood.

"What exactly do you want from this?" Suzie asked. "I mean, why now?"

I felt the prickle of tears. How could I explain that I still heard the heart that beat above me for nine months? I wanted to see the woman whose blood ran through my veins. I wanted to see who I looked like. "I don't know. I think I just want to see that she's alive and okay."

Originally, I'd wanted to ask her why she gave me up, but that question was moot now. How could she have kept me? What I now wanted to know most of all was what had happened to her. How had she ended up in prison, pregnant, serving a life sentence?

"Back then women didn't have the choices they do now," Suzie said.

"I'm not judging her," I said. "I just want to know more about what happened."

My mom used to sing Beatles songs to me when I was a baby. I guess that's why she could never let go of the John Lennon thing. I spent my first ten years in Englewood, New Jersey. Tree-lined streets and nuclear families. We moved to San Francisco when my dad got a job managing a West Coast division of the chemical company he'd worked for since college. Other than the divorce, my life had seemed as flat as a well-ironed shirt. Even the discovery that I was a lesbian was no big deal. I was fourteen when it occurred to me that I was one of a tiny minority of eighth grade girls whose dream date was not Leonardo diCaprio. I immediately found the only other girl in my dorm on my wavelength and we soon figured out we were batting for the Queer Nation.

I never suffered a moment of anxiety about my sexuality. Courtney and I kept quiet about our newly discovered identities as genuine rebels and social misfits. The nuns were not crazy about "special friendships," and we didn't want to be sent home in disgrace. So we enjoyed our anti-establishment status and practiced our sexual technique in the privacy of our respective dorm bedrooms whenever it seemed safe to do so, but we didn't spend enough time alone together for anyone to notice our attachment.

I still saw Courtney sometimes. She was now a vegan environmentalist, and she and her girlfriend had a tree house among the redwoods in the Russian River valley. They had invited me to stay there any time I wanted to get away from it all.

Apart from my dad's lapse with the beauty queen, the only source of angst in my first twenty years was the knowledge that I was adopted. I knew my parents loved me. I knew being adopted didn't mean I was less than flesh and blood to them. But I felt strangely incomplete, as if I had lost my memory and been washed up on a beach where nice people took care of me but I would forever wonder if I should have been leading a different life with different people. Did God send us to our birth mothers with a plan in mind, only to have this subverted when some of us were seen as "mistakes"? Every time Suzie and I talked about whether lesbians should give a shit about Roe versus Wade, I felt a nagging unease.

"I've always wondered why she didn't have an abortion," I said. I used to wonder, if she'd wanted me enough to go through with the pregnancy, why did she give me away? At least I had the answer to that question now.

"I think it's a good idea to try and find her. Obviously it's been weighing on your mind. If there's anything I can do to help, just tell me." Suzie gave me a quick cuddle and, sensitive to my mood, changed the topic to something that wouldn't make my eyes sting. "Hey, did I tell you? I'm writing a lesbian vampire novel."

"How original." Layla's face instantly came to mind, my blood dripping from her chin.

"I think vampires are sexy. I mean, *The Hunger*. Oh, my God. And the books are really popular."

"I wonder why that is," I mused in a disingenuous singsong. "Let's see. Could it be the sad clichés, the cloned characters, the derivative plot, the dopey mythology purloined from whatever flavor-of-the-month spiritual tradition sounds cool. Hey, I know…maybe you could write Kabbalist vampires. Has anyone done that?"

"You're such a bookstore snob," Suzie said. "But since you mention it, vampires *could* fit into the Kabbalist worldview. There's quite a dovetail with that philosophy, as a matter of fact."

I snickered. "How would you know?"

"I've been seeing one," Suzie said with a sanctimonious little sniff.

"A vampire?"

"Oh, ha ha."

"I thought you were with Jordan again." Jordan was one of Suzie's on-again off-again fuck buddies. The last time I saw her she was dealing Ecstasy to pay for her Scientology sessions. Before that, she was an activist for PETA.

"Well, she's into Kabbalism now and we talked about my book plan. She has an interesting perspective. I think Kabbalism is really helping her."

I didn't say the first thought in my head, which was that getting a real job and cutting her consumption of designer drugs by, say, 90 percent could help her too. I thought Jordan was bad for Suzie. "I'm happy for her," I sniped.

"Liar. You don't like her."

"I never said that."

"You don't have to."

"Okay. I just think you could do better, that's all. You're too good for her."

"You're right," Suzie agreed. "But you know what they say…"

"Girls just want to have fun?"

"No…if you can't be with the one you love, love the one you're with." Like she'd just had an epiphany, Suzie got bouncy. "Hey, wanna go to Kinky Salon for Halloween? Karla can get us in."

"Karla?" I tried to imagine preppy Karla in a zip-front latex dress and decided I'd pay money to see that. Her breasts were legendary. On the other hand, what could I wear that wouldn't look completely ridiculous? "It's not exactly our crowd."

"How do you know? You've never been."

"Have you?"

"Once or twice."

Who knew? "You never said anything to me."

"I was going to, but I forgot."

Suzie thought I had hang-ups. She never told me the really outrageous stuff. Wanting to sound like I was finally leaving Catholic school behind me, I said, "I'm not sure if I'll be in town, but if I am, I'll come."

"Really?" She was genuinely surprised.

I was pretty confident that I would not be called upon to keep this bold promise. "So long as I don't have to dress up in a rabbit suit or anything," I said cheerfully.

"I don't think the furry crowd will be there," Suzie assured me. "I'm going to go as a vampire huntress."

Just what the world needs—another Buffy. "You could take Eric along and slay him every so often," I said. "I'll bring the stakes."

Suzie frowned at me. "What is it with you two?"

"Ask him."

"I have. He told me you did him a favor with the pretend fiancée trip and he tried to do one back for you but it bombed."

"Interesting version of the facts."

"Whatever. I just wish you'd work it out. I hate that my two favorite people aren't talking."

I gave a nonchalant shrug. "You'll get over it."

❖

There I was, sitting at the computer on yet another Friday night, making myself crazy by staring at Reverie's dead user icon. I couldn't help wondering if the reason she vanished was that she didn't like my pic, but most of the time, I just felt angry with her. We'd been friends. The least she could do was say a final good-bye to me like our connection had counted for something.

The doorbell rang, not unusual for a Friday night, only this time it wasn't the pizza guy or Peaches wanting to drag me to a party.

"Eric." I was stupidly happy to see him but managed to conceal this fact with a scowl.

He got down on his knees and said, "What will it take? I normally don't offer to lick boots unless the circumstances are very special, but in your case I could make an exception."

I plucked at his shoulder. "Get up before my neighbor sees you and invites himself over."

"Ah, yes. The queen who saved you from bondage gone bad." He stood and dusted off the knees of his faded jeans. As usual he looked like he'd just stepped away from a Calvin Klein fashion shoot.

I stuck my hands on my hips so I would not grab him and kiss him. Only now did I get how much I'd missed him. "What are you doing here?" I said discouragingly. "It's almost midnight."

"I come bearing gifts." He produced a couple of small packages. "Are you going to invite me in or make me stand out here in the snow?"

I looked up at the November sky. "It's not snowing."

"I was painting a poetic picture of my angst, you Philistine."

"Okay." I stepped aside. "You can come in out of the cold, but only because I'm pitying MBAs this week."

He grinned and headed for his usual loitering spot, leaning on my kitchen counter, all set for me to do what I always used to do when he was here in the wee hours, which was make decaf Irish coffee and brownies.

I put the kettle on and said, "Gifts, huh?"

He slid the two packages across the counter. I opened the first and was happy to see an ounce of premium weed. I sniffed inside the baggie and happily exclaimed, "Awesome."

The second offering was a small leather box like the one my fake engagement ring came in. I hoped Eric wasn't so insensitive that he was giving it to me as a souvenir of that sordid week. There was a card with it so I opened that first, staving off the moment of truth. I wasn't up for abject dismay, and I'd already thrown the ring at his feet once. I didn't want to have to do it again.

The card had a picture of Greta Garbo on it. Inside, the caption *I Want To Be Alone* had been amended with the insertion of *Don't* written in red. Eric had scrawled below this:

> *Please forgive me for being a thoughtless, selfish, duplicitous heel. I would give anything to go back in time and change what I did so you wouldn't be hurt. I miss you. Please accept this small gift as a token of my groveling self-abasement and pitiful desire to be accepted back into your life.*
>
> *Your friend,*
> *Eric*
> *(the guy who would marry you, if fags married dykes)*

I refused to look at him. The words were blurry and my throat was sore from holding back tears. Since my heated conversation with Layla, it had occurred to me that I had gone along with the initial deception of my own free will. Eric was not the only person responsible for what had happened in the end. I opened the box and stared down at a really amazing necklace. A string of small transparent purple beads held a pendant made of silver and gold. It was like a half-closed lotus and to one side of the center was a glimmering pinkish orange stone.

"What is it?" I asked, lifting this lovely creation from its black velvet cushion.

"A padparadscha sapphire," he said. "They call that color lotus blossom. It's supposed to make the wearer wise and intuitive."

Since I needed all the help I could get in that department, I fastened the pendant around my neck. It sat just below the base of my throat, perfect for wearing with a T-shirt. I said, "I hope it wasn't really expensive or anything."

"Don't worry, it's not an Asscher diamond."

"I still can't believe your mom was fooled by that ring."

"She wasn't." When I squinted at him, he explained, "It was the real thing."

"Oh, my God. I was wearing an actual diamond? Jesus. What if I'd lost it at the zoo or in the swimming pool?"

"There was no choice. My mother can spot a fake at a hundred paces."

"I figured." The kettle started to hiss and I turned the gas down so I wouldn't have boiling water flying out from under the lid, a side effect of silly but hip design. The kettle was a gift from Suzie.

"I was planning to give the ring to you after it was all over," he said. "As a thank-you. I still have it if you want it."

I touched the pendant. "This is more my kind of thing. Although thanks." I could picture Suzie slapping me upside the head and insisting I accept the genuine diamond so she could wear it home to impress her parents. Out of curiosity, I asked, "What's a diamond ring like that worth?"

"Seventy thousand."

I knew my mouth was hanging open. "You're kidding."

"Insane, isn't it? It's all about supply and demand. The diamond industry holds back enough stones to keep prices artificially high."

"Just like the oil industry?"

"Fruit from the same vines of avarice," he said darkly.

"How do you know all of this?"

"My father used to buy loose stones as an investment. One of our last arguments was over blood diamonds."

I had heard of these. "The ones from places where they finance rebel armies and so on?"

"Exactly. Like Sierra Leone. Diamonds funded their civil war for years. Al Qaeda launders money and helps fund terrorism in places like that by buying blood diamonds."

Amazed to hear Eric talking about something political, I asked, "Did you go to a U2 concert or something?"

He laughed. "I don't live to party. In fact, now that I'm a CEO, I read daily reports from all major media."

"Oh, you've got a new job?"

"You could say that. I even have a secretary. She's the one who sent the packages out to be gift wrapped. She's a cross between a concierge and a confidante."

I looked down at my new pendant and thought about the occasional article I'd seen about kidnapped children forced to work in mines, their arms hacked off or their families butchered if they refused. It made sparkly stones seem much less appealing all of a sudden.

"There aren't any blood sapphires, are there?" I asked.

"You can wear most colored gemstones in good conscience." Eric sounded like a spokesperson for Stick-it-to-De Beers dot org. "Your sapphire came from Sri Lanka. The workers who mine for them get a fair share of the value if they find one."

"That's a good thing, because I really like this necklace." I poured boiling water over some chocolate to melt it, then blended the results into a saucepan of milk.

Eric came over and stirred the mixture while I found marshmallows. "I mean it about missing you," he said. "Can we just kiss and make up now?"

I couldn't resist the pathos in his eyes, and the truth was, I hated not having him for a friend. It seemed really stupid to keep on being angry. I was punishing him, but I was also punishing myself. "I've missed you too." My voice was so husky I had to cough to clear my vocal chords. "I've been stubborn."

"You had every right to be pissed."

"Why did you do it?"

He watched me pour the hot chocolate into mugs and pile on the marshmallows. "I'm going to tell you something." He lowered his voice. "But you have to promise me you'll never say a word about it to anyone."

"Sure. My lips are sealed."

He followed me into the living area and we sat down on my old sofa. Cagily, he said, "I was trying to protect my mother."

I frowned, perplexed. "How exactly was finding me in bed with Layla going to protect your mother?"

He took a slow, deep breath like he was about to swear an oath on the witness stand. Again he reiterated, "Remember, you can't tell a soul."

"My word is my bond," I rashly declared. It was a sordid fact that I had never been very good at keeping secrets, but with more practice I thought I could probably improve on past performance.

"Well, since you're not the leader of the free world, that means something," Eric said. "Fact one—Layla isn't my cousin, she's my half-sister."

I sputtered some marshmallow foam and wiped my mouth with my fingers. I had no idea where Eric was heading with this startling disclosure, but he had my undivided attention. I kept my mouth shut and listened.

"My dad had a relationship with Layla's mom. Mother never knew about it and it would have stayed that way except for Dad's attitude toward me. He made a new will, you see. In it, he left everything to my mother and Layla."

"So this was all about money." Just as I'd suspected.

"No," he protested. "I didn't care who he left his money to. The thing is, he wrote a letter of explanation to go with the will."

I could feel my brain straining to tie these facts together to explain why Layla had slept with me. "What happened to the letter?"

"Wait. Here's how cunning the old man was." Bitterness invaded Eric's voice. "He told me all about the will not long after I came out to him. He said if I didn't straighten myself out, so to speak, I'd end up with nothing."

"What a trip." I could see now why Eric had mixed feelings about his father. "That's some nasty emotional blackmail."

"I told him I didn't care about the money. God, he hated that." Eric lapsed into reflection.

I could tell he was still wounded, and I could relate. My father had also betrayed me and my mother. The difference was, he'd never stopped loving me and in the end, we talked about what had happened. He apologized for hurting me and I forgave him and let go of my anger. It only cost ten thousand bucks for six months of family therapy to reach this milestone. Money well spent, both my parents said. I wished Eric and his father had done something like that, but there are men who will never go to therapy. My mom said it was because they had to be right about everything. I had a feeling Eric's father was one of these.

I touched his hand. "I wish you'd had a chance to talk to him again."

"I wish we could have had a real conversation while he was still okay," Eric said with resigned sorrow. "But Dad wasn't a good listener. It was his way or the highway."

"I don't get it." I hesitated to sound like I didn't buy his story or understand his feelings, but something didn't add up. "If you didn't care about the money, why did you want to go through with the fake engagement?"

"Ah, yes. Well, here's the kicker." Eric lifted his movie-star eyes to mine and treated me to an expression full of injured pride, exactly the same one I'd seen on Layla's face a few nights earlier. No wonder they were spookily alike. "Last year Dad finally realized I meant it about the money, so he had to find something else he could hold over me."

I held my breath waiting to hear what else this stupid, homophobic man had done to destroy his son's love for him. And, indeed, there was more.

"That was when he told me about his affair with Aunt Sara and about Layla. He said he'd put it all in a letter to be read with his new will. He said Mother would never forgive Aunt Sara and their relationship would be ruined. The family would never be the same again and it would be my fault."

"That's horrible. I'm sorry, but your father sounds like an asshole."

"He changed," Eric said sadly. "I don't think he would have done something like that normally. But he had a brain tumor. Over time it made him paranoid and mean."

"So the letter was the real issue?"

"I didn't want my mother to know about the affair. She'd be so humiliated; she thought they had the perfect marriage. And Aunt Sara isn't a strong person. I really think it would have killed her if Mother found out."

"She should have thought about that before she cheated with your Dad."

Eric sighed. "She was dating Dad before he married Mother, and I think she was still in love with him. I don't know the full circumstances but I do know my father. He always got what he wanted."

"So, now I guess everyone knows." I felt sorry for his family and disgusted that we'd almost lost our friendship over a cunning plan that didn't pay off in the end anyway.

"Actually…not quite." Eric took a heavy sheet of parchment paper from the inside pocket of his jacket, unfolded it, and handed it to me, inviting, "Read clause nine."

I dutifully read a long paragraph of incomprehensible legalese. "What does it mean?"

"It instructs my mother that if Dad is terminally ill and dies, and I am either engaged or married and she believes that I will have children, she is to sign an affidavit to that effect and the attorney will destroy all documents in an envelope marked A."

"Don't tell me…Envelope A contained the letter and the will that disinherited you?"

"Yes. And there was an Envelope B. It contained a will leaving the business to me and all the matrimonial assets to Mother."

"And no letter?"

"No letter."

"So it was your mom we had to persuade all along? The reconciliation with your dad was just a red herring."

He looked fittingly shamed. "Yes. I thought if I told you the whole story, you'd be more nervous with her than you already were."

"Your mother never knew anything about the wills?"

"No. She was really offended when the probate attorney started asking questions about my sexuality. She told him it didn't matter who I was with so long as I was happy."

"That's great!" It was good to know his mom would come down on his side if the heat was on. That's what mothers were supposed to do.

He smiled. "I think she finds it easier to defend me now."

"Because she thinks you're a bisexual instead of completely gay?"

"She's always wanted to believe that. We just gave her permission to convince herself."

"I felt bad letting her think we wanted kids."

"It wasn't a complete lie. I'd like kids one day."

"You would?" I tried to imagine Eric with a sticky-fingered toddler and laughed.

"Now that I can afford the perfect British nanny, I might think about it," he said. "You know something bizarre—Mother thought the questions the lawyer asked were directed at her...that the old man was trying to punish her somehow. She said he'd always blamed her for my sexuality...for making me a Mommy's boy. The usual shit. You should have heard her telling the lawyer how the old man was barking up the wrong tree about everything. She was incensed."

I could imagine Mrs. Standish outraged to have her maternal competence called into question. I would not have wanted to be that lawyer. Sipping my chocolate, I sorted the facts into a story I could make sense of. Eric had embarked on our charade to protect his mother and his family. I had a hard time finding fault in that, even if I didn't like my own role.

"Did Layla know about the will and the letter?"

"No. And she has no idea about Dad."

I recalled her poolside comments about waiting for her "uncle" to die. How ironic. "So, she slept with me because you asked her to help you get out of the engagement."

"I sold her the idea that I was in over my head and I needed a way out. But all I asked her to do was make it look compromising. I had no idea how far she was going to take it."

My breathing got erratic. "She didn't plan on having sex with me?"

"No. But you two seemed to hit it off, and frankly..." He hesitated like he wanted to confide something, but could not find the words. "I thought you might be good for her too."

"You were matchmaking?"

"Kind of."

I put my hot chocolate on the coffee table and rested my forehead in my palm. Eric's dad had wanted to control his family from the grave. Eric's mom lived in denial. Layla had no idea that her birth father had died and she'd almost inherited a big company. I thought about her cynical remark...that Eric had walked away with everything he wanted. She was right.

"Do you feel guilty that Layla inherited nothing?" I asked, keeping my tone neutral. To me it seemed wrong. "He was her father."

"No, he wasn't," Eric said without missing a beat. "Their connection was nothing more than an accident of genetics. To be a father, a man has to do more than fertilize an egg."

"But doesn't the law say illegitimate children have a claim on the estates of their birth parents?"

"If Layla didn't have her trust fund, I'd definitely feel responsible and I'd definitely give her a fair share. But if I tried to do that now, it would open a can of worms. For a start, she'd want to know why, and everything would come out."

"Bad idea," I conceded.

"On top of that, it could be argued that Layla should hand back all the money she inherited when her own dad died. He had a son from his first marriage. Technically, that kid could say Layla's trust fund belongs to him."

I could not imagine having problems like these. "Shit like this can only happen to rich people," I said.

"There are millionaires in your line of work. You'd better watch out or you'll be next."

"We're too political. Look what the Dixie Chicks have had to put up with."

"You're not trying to sell CDs to rednecks." He surveyed me affectionately and it dawned on me that, having inherited the company, Eric might have to give up the new job he was so pleased about.

"What are you going to do now?" I asked. "Can you stay in your new job and still take charge of the family business?"

He gave me a duh! look. "Sweetie, my new job is the family business. I'm the CEO of Standish Industrial now."

"Does that mean you're stuck in San Diego?"

"Only when I have to be at board meetings. Most of the time I work remotely, and we have offices in other cities, so there's a lot of travel."

"Are you happy?"

He grinned. "I'm having a blast. I know the old man would hate it but I'm going to drag his company into the twenty-first century and I won't have to sack half the workforce to do it."

He rambled on to me about a public float and purchasing smaller rivals, and a big investment in alternative energy. He wanted to diversify into future technologies, especially in the medical area. He was about to buy a stake in a stem cell research company in South Korea.

He was so certain of himself, so driven and happy, I couldn't tell him not to become a disconnected elitist. "Don't wait too long between visits," I said.

"Layla said the same thing." He paused. "She tells me you two brokered a truce."

"We agreed to disagree and move on."

"Fabulous." He seized one of my hands and planted a big kiss on the knuckles.

"Don't get too excited," I cautioned. I could see him counting chickens before they hatched. "She made it very clear she isn't looking for a relationship."

"So, change her mind," he said, like I was missing some vital part of the equation. "All's fair in love and war. You need a strategy."

"Even if I had one, I wouldn't be around to implement it," I said. "We're recording our album pretty soon and after that Mr. Goldman says we're going on the road. As in, for months."

"Suzie and I need to be in the front row for your first major gig," he said. "Plus a backstage pass and the band party afterward."

I said, "I'll tell my people," and we both snorted with laughter.

"Just don't turn into a wanker," Eric warned when we'd settled down. "That's British for being a pretentious jerkoff."

"I'll try to remain unspoiled by fame," I replied solemnly.

"Layla thinks you're going be one of the singers of the decade."

"People say stuff like that to build my confidence."

"Give her some credit. She's a professional."

I sighed. "Sometimes she seems so…sad. Do you know what that's about?"

He gave a helpless shrug. "It's not my story to tell."

"So, there is a story?"

"Everyone has a story." His face was unusually somber. "Layla has a novel."

CHAPTER TWELVE

The recording studio was a sea of lights and switches and wires. We occupied what felt like a glass bubble. Beyond this, people wearing headphones were crammed into a tiny room.

One of the sound engineers had worked with Jimi Hendrix on the epic "Voodoo Child" track in 1968, Mr. Goldman told us. He owned an original 1952 Fender Telecaster which various legendary guitarists had borrowed during recording sessions. This got Peaches more excited than front row tickets to Green Day. It was her dream to own such a vintage guitar, we discovered, as she and the gray haired chief engineer bonded. They spent at least an hour agreeing that Keith Richards is the greatest rhythm guitar player who ever lived and speculating on whether his pairing with Mick Taylor was musically more important than the weave of lead and rhythm he developed with Ron Wood.

Once we were done with all the sound testing and cue mix adjustments, Mr. Goldman returned to the tiny room with the technical people and spoke to us over an intercom. Our task was to record a bunch of songs from which we would make the final selections for our debut album. We would then lay down numerous extra voice and instrumental tracks and somehow all of this material would be blended into songs with every sonic nuance polished just as the engineer decreed it should be.

Peaches decided we would start with one of her songs, "Past in Flames," about a woman who gets out of an abusive relationship and goes back to burn the family home down with her ex-husband inside. Mr. Goldman wasn't crazy about it, but he thought it would work for the album. It took about twenty attempts to get as far as the first chorus.

We would be here for weeks, I thought.

Amazingly, by late in the afternoon we'd managed to record three songs and Mr. Goldman wanted us to do one of Layla's before we took a break. I felt anxious right away. Most of Peaches's songs were guitar-driven, whereas Layla's, with their slower blues rhythms, exposed my creaking vocals.

Stomach lurching, I scanned the lyrics to "Equinox," a ballad Mr. Goldman happily described as a one-listen song. I eased into the first verse, struck as always by the song's simplicity and emotional impact. Layla had written "Equinox" in New Orleans, during what she termed her "blue period." It dealt with a woman trying to make sense of her lover's suicide so she could get on with her own life. I had pumped Eric for more information about this tale, without success. He said Layla's life was full of bizarre happenings and he wasn't at liberty to discuss them. According to him, she was just as easily inspired to creativity by some hard-luck story she read in a newspaper as she was by her own personal dramas.

The chorus of the song was punctuated with a plaintive electric violin—Mr. Goldman's idea. I managed to come in on time and hold my final note long enough to make it to the next verse. Peaches gave me the thumbs-up and played an immaculate lead guitar riff, and for the first time since I'd started singing with the band I felt a sense of connectedness, like we were all intensely aware of one another and plugged into the same wavelength. We sounded like a band instead of five individuals.

We finished the session and hugged one another. Mr. Goldman rewound the tape and played it back. Everyone was blown away. The chief engineer said we still had a lot of work to do. This was evidently a compliment.

It took another two months to complete our album. In that time Mr. Goldman sent tapes of our most promising singles to a bunch of radio stations and to my complete astonishment, I tuned into SomaFM one evening and heard my own voice. There's nothing quite like that feeling. I sounded like a stranger, more gravely than in the studio. I thought this was possibly the effect of breathing L.A. smog for weeks on end while we were recording. We'd also played a series of minor but hip venues in Southern California, and had started getting some attention from fringe media.

Soma's DJ Elise described us as a hot new sound and mentioned our soon-to-be-released album. Not long after this "key exposure," Mr. Goldman started a rumor that Siren was dating a fellow drummer from a Seattle grunge band and Peaches got arrested for possession of cocaine. Mr. Goldman sent her to rehab for a couple of weeks so she could rub shoulders with celebrities. We attended power-schmooze sessions at places like Barney's Beanery, under instructions to look sexy but disinterested.

Then we got the phone call Mr. Goldman had been hanging out for. KEXP Seattle liked "Equinox." So did KROQ. Within days, over two hundred radio stations had added the song to their playlist, a process we later discovered was lubricated by pay-for-play incentives from Mr. Goldman's label. Who knew that stations didn't select songs for their merit and that air time was owned by those who could pay for it? I'd always felt there had to be an explanation for Britney Spears and Jessica Simpson, and here it was.

At the time, we had no clue about the payola principle and lost our minds when our album, named for Peaches's song "Past In Flames," pre-sold 150,000 units. *People* magazine identified us as the next big thing and compared me with Chrissie Hynde. As if. We read in *Rolling Stone* that we'd turned down an offer to pose nude for *Playboy*.

That's how fast it happened. Photo shoots. Interviews. Parties. Gigs. And, of course, MTV and VH1. Suddenly we had a manager and lawyers and bank accounts full of money advanced to us by Mr. Goldman. Peaches got a diamond barbell for her pierced navel. Siren bought a new Harley. Lucrezia paid for her mom to go on a cruise. Bella made the cover of *Ebony*. I had to resign my grooming job and Mrs. Van Wynterhaven gave me a photo of herself with Princess Sofia and Drak, the Borzoi, as a farewell gift.

Virgin Blessing hit the road, playing at every alternative venue from Seattle to N.Y.C. until, six months later, we were opening for big-name bands. We had our own blog and a fan club set up by one of Lucrezia's admirers, a man who described himself as wanting to be her boot-licking slave. She said he meant that literally.

I looked at myself in the mirror every morning and wondered who I was anymore. I could feel myself changing. It was like aliens visited me in my sleep and entered new data into my brain. I would wake up and know for sure that another tiny shift had occurred; the furniture of my mind had been rearranged again.

Every so often, I wondered if I was turning into the wanker Eric had warned me about. *Metamorphosis*. A new creature was emerging, just like in Kafka's story. I was alarmed, excited, disbelieving. Was I just growing up more, or was something sinister happening? I felt helpless, like I was on the outside looking in. I didn't understand the process and I wasn't even sure if it was really taking place at all or if I was just tired, introspective and indulging in too many recreational drugs.

I didn't have a habit; it was more of a hobby. I had no time for junkies and no plans to become one. I was careful and only scored from the same trustworthy dealer all the time. Peaches and Siren were into coke and acid, and sometimes they were so wasted we couldn't practice. That made Bella and Lucrezia mad. They never got high while we were working and only smoked weed when we weren't. Mostly, I hung with them, especially Luke, who had become my closest friend in the band. Sometimes I scored from her; she had friends who grew specialty weed indoors. This made me a dope snob. I could discuss the merits of various strains and came up with hybrid concepts I thought growers should consider. I could identify the different highs of Silver Haze and Northern Lights and the Nepalese Temple Ball flavor of Flo.

Luke and I would get high together and have extremely long, philosophical conversations about music and life, then fall asleep on furniture. Or we would drink instead, and go out and pick up women. Neither of us liked getting really drunk and Luke thought alcohol impaired her performance in the sack so she tended to nurse one drink all evening and was always the designated driver. I found that alcohol helped me get over inhibitions and Catholic guilt, so I tended to drink too much and go home trashed, without picking up anyone.

Sometimes, if we were partying at someone's house after a gig, I would dip into my Ecstasy cache. I liked to grind up a couple of pills, split a brownie in half and sprinkle on the happy powder, then sandwich the halves back together and divide the brownie. I would eat half and be energized and thrilled by the world for hours, then spend some time chilling and getting hydrated, and then I would eat the other half and have busy, intense sex with whoever.

At those times I would think about Layla and wonder where she was and what she was doing and whether she ever thought about me.

I had followed Eric's advice and adopted a strategy. I phoned her after gigs and told her how much the crowd loved her songs and how thankful I was that she wrote the way she did, so I sounded better than I really was. She was always nice to me, but distant.

I sent her flowers fairly often, because Eric had told me she liked lilies and orchids. She would e-mail polite, funny thank-you notes to me, the kind that reminded me we were on a friendly, platonic footing. Every now and then I got pissed off and would write her a long e-mail, pouring out my thoughts about various shit that happened in the band and my endless disappointment that the guys I'd hired to find my birth mother kept coming up empty-handed. Lightly and carefully, I would hint that I'd like us to be closer. I always told her if she ever needed to talk, I was here. She never took me up on the offer.

I wanted to get Luke's take on my strategy, since she was older and highly successful with women, but she didn't seem to like Layla, so I would ask general questions that could be about any woman. She would say things like: "Face-to-face is always the best plan. Tell her you can't get her out of your mind and ask her what it's going to take for her to say yes."

When I got really morose, she would tell me, "Sometimes it just isn't going to happen. Maybe you need to accept that and move on."

I would listen to these pearls of wisdom and wish I were more like her. Luke had something. In her universe, women never said no; they said please.

I talked to Suzie on the phone all the time, from motels and houses of friends of the band, cheap hotels and the minibus Mr. Goldman had purchased for us. She and Eric showed up for a few of our gigs, sometimes as a surprise. Increasingly, I found myself pining for home and my parents and normal life. I wanted to wake up alone, wearing my old cotton T-shirt, and go to the bathroom and read the *People* magazines I kept by the door. I wanted to brush my teeth and poke around in my fridge and lean on the counter going through my appointment book.

I felt like my life in San Francisco was a photograph, everything in the same place, but a blur in the middle where I used to be.

CHAPTER THIRTEEN

S iren showed up late to my birthday party. She had a black eye. It wasn't the first time.

Bella said, "Girl, you all right?"

"I don't want to talk about it, okay?" Siren handed a big box of Godiva chocolates to me.

Bella cast a glance in Luke's direction, and Luke said, "Where is he?"

Siren shook her head. "Just leave it alone. Please."

I could tell she'd been crying up a storm and hugged her, thanking her for the present and distracting her with happy chatter about the great new tattoo on her nape and the food Suzie was cooking in the kitchen.

We'd converted Mrs. Goldman's basement into a recording studio with a huge apartment. The place was soundproof and Mr. Goldman liked that we were there a lot so we could check on his mom. Suzie was catering the party. She'd finally turned her cooking hobby into a real business and even had employees. We gave her business cards to everyone and hired her whenever we had to lay on fancy appetizers to impress media and the rich people who owned a piece of Mr. Goldman's label.

I let my eyes drift past Siren's shoulder and met Luke's eyes. Her face showed little expression but she was as angry as I'd ever seen her; I could tell from her body language and the tight line of her mouth. She and Bella were having a conversation that comprised looks, frowns, and terse whispers.

Peaches joined me and Siren in a three-way hug and said, "Babe, you can't keep going back to him. You know that, don't you?"

Siren looked so disillusioned I wanted to take her somewhere beautiful just so she could smile. "I thought it would be different this time," she said. "He was clean for eight weeks."

"I'm sorry." Peaches stroked her hair and we led her through a jostling sea of people I barely knew to a private corner of the room where she could pull herself together.

As we walked, I whispered in Peaches's ear, "Don't let her go back there tonight."

"Tell Luke it's time," Peaches whispered back.

"Time?"

"Just tell her."

Dutifully, I nudged my way through the crowd, pausing to receive air kisses and gushy congratulations. I found Luke in the kitchen watching Suzie drop little blobs of caviar on tiny pastry boats filled with pale goo that probably had a French name. Screened by the open pantry door, I stood in the doorway, arrested by the sight. Luke was leaning against one end of the long servery counter, her expression indulgent. She wore loose, faded blue 501 jeans and a plain white shirt with the sleeves rolled up over her muscular forearms. Her thick matte black leather belt matched her boots. The buckle was simple and heavy, a pewter one she often wore.

I had no idea how she could look so sexual in such ordinary clothes, but Luke exuded a primal vibe no one could miss. Even gay men checked her out.

Suzie's cheeks were pink and she was giggling. Luke smiled a lazy, knowing smile and all of a sudden I was breathing hard and couldn't swallow. Suzie lifted one of her creations and popped it into Luke's mouth. I was outraged.

"God, that's good," Luke sighed after consuming the morsel. "Lobster mousse...and is that fennel?"

"Yes! No one ever guesses that combination. You have quite a palate."

"You're a terrific cook."

Was Luke flirting with my best friend? It was one thing to discard groupies like used guitar strings, but if our resident heartbreaker thought she could chew Suzie up and spit her out, she could think again.

I stepped into the room, interrupting their cozy banter. "Hey, Luke, can I have a word?"

"Sure." Her eyes swept over me and I was quite sure I detected a glitter of lust in their depths.

I wanted to slap her. Unwanted images of her and Suzie leapt into my mind. I could see them kissing. I pictured Luke taking the ribbons from Suzie's pigtails and moving her hand beneath Suzie's skirt. Horrible!

Suzie surveyed me, and a small innocent frown wrinkled her brow. "Want a lobster mousse boat?" she offered.

When I shook my head, she waved to one of her waiters and the young woman straightened her white apron over her black pants and picked up a tray of the awesome lobster pastries.

"Enjoying your party?" Luke asked me.

I shrugged. Mr. Goldman had invited a horde of booking agents, session musicians, fans, and industry people. I'd seen some of them around, but most were strangers. Virgin Blessing would play later, supposedly an impromptu jam. He said it was all about the right kind of exposure. I took his word for it and made nice to everyone.

"I was telling Lucrezia about Kinky Salon," Suzie said perkily. "She says she'll take me if you don't want to go."

Oh, I just bet she will! I could hardly form a response. Suzie looked like she was loving the idea. "That won't be necessary." I ground the words out like my lips were made of sandpaper. "I think I'll be in town."

"Then we can all go," Suzie chirped. "Oh, wow. I can hardly wait."

I was about ready to grab a handful of cocktail olives and throw them on the floor, when Luke said, "You wanted me, Chance?"

The softly spoken question made the hairs on the back of my neck stand up. I hated that after all these months of us being buddies, I still read double entendre into half the things she said.

Suzie compounded my angst by choosing that moment to joke, "I know what you want! You've come for your birthday kiss." To Luke, she announced, "She told me she was going to proposition you."

I knew my face was scarlet. My cheeks were so hot the kitchen lights felt like sun lamps. I thought I glimpsed a speculative glint in Luke's eyes, but it was gone before I could be certain and with her customary sangfroid, she responded, "Feel free. Everyone else does."

I mock scowled at her, then gave Suzie a playful shove, like I was in on the joke. "Troublemaker."

Suzie sighed melodramatically. "Looks like she doesn't want you." She sidled over to Luke, full of sass. "You'll just have to settle for me."

"I'm used to it." Luke grinned. "I can't even get to first base with her."

"As if," I snorted, dismayed that she was playing along with Suzie, teasing the birthday girl.

If I were brutally honest, it also bothered me that Luke had never actually tried to get to first base. Not that I wanted her to hit on me. I didn't have sex with my friends. But occasionally I wondered what I would do if she made a move on me.

I pushed my hair back from my forehead so it wouldn't be obvious that I was looking her up and down, and with a shock, I realized I would totally crumble. If Luke kissed me right now, I would not only kiss her in return but probably want more. I was mortified. Was I not getting enough sex that I was prone to lurid fantasies about my friends? Had someone slipped a pill into my beer?

I dragged my traitorous gaze away from the crotch of Luke's jeans and inspected the canapés on the counter with the kind of fascination normally reserved for food with the face of the Virgin Mary on it. All the while I was aware of Luke and Suzie standing in body contact, acting like everything was completely fine and they could just go right ahead and flirt with each other in front of me.

I refocused my thoughts on my mission. I still hadn't passed Peaches's coded message on to Luke. Here was the perfect excuse to get her away from Suzie before something dire happened. At the rate they were going, they would be out of here at the end of Suzie's catering shift and heading back to her place. Tomorrow I would hear all about how great Luke was in bed.

Not amused by *that* possibility, I said, "It's about Siren. Want to talk in the den?"

We'd learned to have our own private parties within parties and had built a small den out the back when the basement was remodelled, a room we could escape to with our closest friends.

"Good idea." Luke's eyes lingered on Suzie for a second too long and she said, "I hope it pans out with the new chef, Suzie. Catch you later."

As we squeezed past the party animals, I said crankily, "Are you into Suzie?"

"No," Luke said with mild amusement. "Why?"

How was I supposed to answer that without sounding like one of those interfering people who can't let their friends live their own lives? Luke wouldn't put up with that kind of crap for a minute. Making a big effort to appear casual, I said, "Just asking."

She measured me with a cool stare. "You seemed jealous back there. What's up with that? Are *you* into her?"

"No. She's my best friend, that's all. I don't want her getting hurt."

Luke opened the door and we entered the den. We'd kept some of Mrs. Goldman's unwanted furniture in there. It made the place feel more like a home. "Hurt," she echoed. "You mean by me?"

Who else? I dropped into an armchair and stuck my feet on the ancient coffee table. "She's not a toy."

Luke's face grew serious. "You have nothing to worry about. I like Suzie but she's not my type."

I wanted to be mollified by this, but I still felt agitated and I couldn't stop thinking of Luke with Suzie. In fact, with several of the women out there. She was bound to choose one of them to take home. She always scored more easily with the interesting ones than I did. For some reason the thought bothered me more than usual.

Was I envious? If so, that was pathetic. Determined to get a hold of myself, I said, "Peaches wanted me to tell you it's time."

"Ah." This obscure message evidently meant something to her. She took her cell phone from her belt, excused herself and went out onto our little deck. Ignoring the cool weather, she stood there talking for a minute or two.

I took that opportunity to reflect on my irrational behavior. So what if she and Suzie were flirting? It didn't have to mean anything. And she'd just told me she wasn't interested. Luke never lied about that stuff. Nothing was happening, so there was no reason for me to feel fretful.

I stared at her through the glass-paneled door and reminded myself that Luke was a good friend to me and a good person. The least I could do was behave accordingly. I gave her a big smile as she came back into the room and was gratified to see her expression soften. She came over

---

and sat on the sofa opposite me.

"I need to go out for a while," she said. "I want you to make sure Siren stays here."

"Sure. What are you doing?"

"Getting her stuff and having that jerk arrested."

"She won't talk to the cops." We'd been through this before when he broke two of her ribs. For a smart, attractive, talented woman, Siren was amazingly stupid when it came to males.

"She won't need to," Luke said with calm assurance. "When we take her stuff, he won't be happy. My guess is he'll throw a punch or two, and when he does, I'll be the one filing charges."

"You can't be serious. You're going to let him hit you?"

"Don't worry. I know how to take care of myself."

"What if he has a gun or a knife?" I was alarmed. "This is crazy."

"The guy I just called...he's a cop and a good friend. He'll be in the vicinity and he's armed."

"I don't like it. You're taking a big risk and for what? All they ever do is give guys like him a fine and a night in the cells."

"Not this time. Peaches told me what's in their house. He's not just a user. He has a meth lab."

What was Siren *thinking*? "You're going to call in the cops and they'll find it?"

"It's in plain sight. All I have to do is give them a reason to enter the apartment."

"That's the bit that worries me."

Luke surprised me by taking my hand. Her cool fingers stroked mine. She smiled at me the way people smile at puppies and children who say things that are unwittingly funny. "This needs to happen and I'll be fine. I'll see you in a few hours. Okay?"

"Okay." On a rash impulse, I leaned forward and kissed her cheek.

For several seconds we stared at one another, then she got to her feet, drawing me up with her. I hated when she let go of my hand. I hated when she strolled away and vanished into the crowd . I had no idea how important she'd become to me until I lost sight of her. Luke was one of the few people in my life I knew I could count on.

❖

My birth mother's name was Mary. My first thought, when the investigator told me, was: at least she's Catholic. That was two months ago and since then "my people" had communicated with "her people," her people being an emphysemic defense attorney with a low-rent walk-up in Mid-Market.

I was waiting on a plastic chair at a Formica table in a visitors room that looked like a disused school classroom and smelled of extra-strength disinfectant. Around me were groups of people trying to behave like this was a normal social situation. I guess for some of them it was.

I told myself that this relatively informal setting with its chirpy Muzak background noise was better than one of those narrow rooms with seats on either side of a bulletproof screen. In here, the prison guards were standing around the walls and wandering between the tables, occasionally stopping to cite a regulation or answer a question. They were all armed with guns and batons and looked scary, although so far I'd found them to be polite in that I-am-the-boss-of-you manner that was the province of the law enforcement fraternity. Maybe they learned it at the police academy, or maybe it just happened once they realized they had the power and everyone had to be really polite to them.

Whatever, it made me nervous, compliant, and paranoid. I don't know how many times I checked myself for evidence of weed before I reached the prison, but I still kept groping inside my pockets.

I supposed criminals were less susceptible than me and had less to lose, so they were less cooperative. I had heard how dangerous and disgusting it could be for guards working in prisons, but I figured the NCWF, being women only, was probably sought-after work. I pictured a sterner version of my boarding school, with worse food and fewer privileges.

As I'd driven there, I marveled that my birth mother had been living only a couple of hours from me for most of my life and I had no idea. The Northern California Women's Facility was located in Stockton, about half an hour south of Sacramento. It was medium security. My mother had been transferred there a few years back from the Valley State Penitentiary in Chowchilla, a dreaded high-security facility, after she provided the state with helpful information about a fellow prisoner.

When the investigator first told me her history, I'd assumed she must be innocent, or failing that, a misled woman who had committed an unspeakable act out of desperation. She had robbed a drug store and shot the clerk in the head. She got away with $300. According to the investigator, she was a junkie, the daughter of a middle-class family, a troublemaker in school who had a rap sheet by the time she was eighteen. Her parents threw her out after she got high and assaulted her mother, and a year later she appeared in the system arrested for prostitution.

I decided this downward spiral must have been caused by sexual abuse at the hands of a male relative or perhaps beatings at home. She had a younger sister, Theresa, who told the investigator that their childhood was normal and uneventful. Theresa was married with two kids, and living in Fresno. She visited my mother several times a year and said that Mary was "doing okay and regretted her crime." My mother had been up for parole for the past eight years but so far the board had turned her down.

This fact added to my certainty that she was the victim of abuse. Everyone knew that in the state of California, women who killed battering husbands in self-defense never got out. It had to be even tougher for those who killed strangers.

A voice announced over the robotic Muzak, "Mary O'Connell," and a heavily built woman in blue denim pants and a lighter blue shirt padded into the room and made a beeline for my table. I stood up. Visitors were allowed to hug the prisoner at the beginning and end of the visit. I had no idea if Mary would want this, but if she did, I was willing. She halted a couple of feet from me and we stared at one another for so long that a guard told us to sit down. The hug didn't happen.

Her hair was short and gray and her eyes were not as green as mine, but I could see something of myself in the set of her eyebrows and the shape of her nose. If I were a junkie now then spent the next thirty years behind bars, I would probably look like her. Mary was only fifty-one, but she looked like she was in her sixties.

I broke the ice by saying, "Thank you for seeing me."

She jerked her head in a nod that was more like a tic and said, "Did you bring the cigarettes like I asked?"

"Yes. And the snacks." I lifted my transparent plastic carry bag onto the table and emptied out a pile of vending-machine purchases. Visitors weren't allowed to bring food into the prison. They let you carry $30 in one dollar bills so you could buy stuff from the machines.

Mary thanked me and gathered the candy and sodas to one side. I'd also bought sandwiches and she tore the packaging from one of these and started eating it. "I wasn't sure if you'd come," she said, chewing fast. "People say they will, but…"

"I wanted to meet you."

She gave a dismissive shrug. "I'm not sure what for."

I had the urge to leave. We were two strangers. There was no sense of connection, and a cloud of private desolation hung so densely about her I doubted the person inside was ever visible. But I had driven here and I didn't want to spend the next ten years wishing I'd asked the questions that bothered me.

"Ever since I was little I've wondered about you," I said.

"Bet you weren't expecting this." She flicked a hand in the direction of a guard. "Did they strip search you coming in?"

"No. They just patted me down and emptied my bag. And they have metal detectors and those wand things, like in airports."

She finished her sandwich and rested both hands on the tabletop. They were pinkish and the skin looked rough. Her nails could have been cleaner. "There's people won't come here because of the strip-searches," she said. "They did that to my sister once and she didn't come back for two years. They strip-search us after visits in case something gets smuggled in."

"I'm sorry." It hadn't crossed my mind that my mother would have to endure this humiliation in order for us to see each other.

"Nothing you can do about it." She dropped her voice and her eyes darted to one of the many wall mounted security cameras. "And it's equal opportunity in the fucking workplace, so you've got male guards standing around while you bend over."

Horrified, I said, "I thought that was illegal."

She laughed, a rasping whoop that suggested lung problems.

I had no idea what to say. I wondered if she was exaggerating. "I spoke to your sister," I said, moving to a more pleasant subject. "She sends her love."

"Be more help if she sent cigarettes." Mary sniffed. "But she wants me to give up."

"Easier said than done."

Again the frenetic nod. "Chantelle. That's classy. Your parents. Are they nice folks?"

I was glad that she had some questions too. "I'm very lucky," I said, wanting her to know the adoption had a positive outcome. I cited the things Suzie thought were worth mentioning. "My parents are really kind people and I grew up in a nice house with plenty of toys. I was an only child."

The woman who had surrendered me to the unknown leaned forward, animated. "When I was a kid I wanted my own room with a TV in it. That was my big dream."

"That's what I had. Pictures on my walls, pretty curtains, a bed with a down comforter. And I had a fine education. I went to private school and college."

"They're rich then, your folks?"

I thought about the Standish mansion and Eric's mom, a woman who had never thought about the cost of a meal or a full tank of gas in her life and thought radiant cut diamonds were vulgar. My parents were not from the same planet. "No, they're not rich. They've worked for what they have."

"I had to give you up," she said in a rush. "You understand that, don't you?"

"Of course. You had no choice."

"I probably wouldn't have kept you, anyway," she reflected. "I couldn't look after a kid back then."

I tried not to be hurt by this. Some part of me badly wanted to hear that she'd have given anything to keep me but I'd prepared myself for the opposite. A woman who committed armed robbery and murder at twenty-three was not in control of her life. At least she knew it was not right to bring a child into that.

"It must have been really hard for you," I said.

"I'll tell you something. Going through the change in this place is fucking hard."

I was aware that she'd intentionally steered the conversation away from the past, and I could sense her jitters and her guilt. She was not the person she'd once dreamed of being, and here I was, a living reminder of a future traded away.

I didn't want to rub her face in what might have been, but I had a right to know some things, so I said, "Can you tell me about my father?"

She blinked rapidly and for a moment I thought she was going to clam up and ask me to leave, but with extreme unease, she said, "I had a regular. A married guy. He was good to me." One of her hands sought the other and her fingers locked together. "I wasn't a hooker. There were men, I don't deny it. And some of them helped me out with cash. But I never turned tricks on street corners. I want you to know that."

I said, "I understand." My father was a john—a man with a wife and family who had purchased sex from a vulnerable young woman and left her pregnant. I felt sick to my stomach.

"He wasn't going to leave his wife. He said he'd pay for an abortion." Her eyes drifted over me and in that second the defeat lifted from her face and I glimpsed a flash of self-respect. "I refused, and here you are."

I reached out and pried her hands apart, taking one of them in mine. "Thank you," I said. "Thank you for giving me life and thank you for making sure I would have a good future."

She burst into tears. "I only did one good thing in my life and you're it."

I looked away as she got herself under control. No one paid us any attention. There had already been several weeping incidents since I'd arrived and I quickly understood that there were tacit rules for how these were handled. They were ignored by the prison population and visitors, and tolerated by the guards.

I listened to the fractured slush of cards being shuffled around us. Something else I'd observed was that people played games to fill silences. No doubt the conversation ran out quickly when you were no longer a part of your children's lives and your partner was probably seeing someone else but claiming he'd wait for you. My mother had been locked up for twenty-eight years. The world had passed her by. Her life was seeping through her fingers and she would never have a chance to grip hold and see where it would take her. She'd made her choice before she had even started.

Gently, I let go of her hand and said, "I have something for you." I lifted my bag onto my knee and fished inside for several items I'd vacillated over bringing. I still wasn't sure if she'd want them, but I thought they'd serve as a distraction. I slid a CD and some photographs across the table. One of the pics was of me and my parents standing in front of their house. The others were shots of me and the band.

My mother pored over the photos then picked up the CD and stared at the jacket.

"I sing in a band," I said. "That's our new CD."

Her cheeks flushed bright red. "You're famous?"

"No, we're just starting out. But our album is doing okay on the charts." I didn't want to make a big deal of it. *Past In Flames* had hit #10, which meant it was "a hot worldwide debut album." But we all avoided mentioning this achievement in case we jinxed ourselves. Occasionally Peaches would bring a news clipping to our weekly band meeting and quietly scream, but we'd made a pact with each other that we wouldn't gloat officially until we had a #1 single or a new artist Grammy nomination. It made me feel good, though, to see Mary's reaction.

Her chest rose and fell with excitement and she kept licking her lips and looking at me in disbelief. Finally, startling me and several guards, she leapt to her feet and called, "Hey, listen up everyone. This here is my daughter and she is in a famous band." Waving the CD, she declared, "This is her record."

Near us, a guard said, "Sit down, O'Connell."

The dronelike din in the room ceased abruptly and we were the focus of hushed scrutiny from all sides. I tugged Mary's arm, but she didn't sit down. She was on a roll and making it up as she went along.

"She's on TV and in the magazines and she knows movie stars. Her band is going to be on *Oprah*."

This got people clapping and a few other prisoners stood up. The pervasive numbness in every face I'd seen since I'd been here, seemed to vanish, supplanted by life and color.

"Let's all just calm down." An older guard moved to the center of the room, men on either side of him. Their hands rested on their guns.

I stood up and put an arm around my mother. Waving acknowledgment to the crowd like I was onstage, I said, "Thank you, everyone. Good to be here. Thank you."

As I urged Mary into her chair, someone called, "Play the CD," and the older officer took a few steps closer.

I could feel the hair rising on the back of my neck as he extended his hand. I made myself a promise that if I walked out of this place without being arrested on suspicion of something, I would never carry drugs on my person again.

"Want me to put it on for you, O'Connell?" He indicated the CD.

My mother gave him a look of timid apprehension.

"You'll get it back," he said and took it from her hand.

I thought she was going to have a heart attack when the Muzak stopped and my voice filtered into the room. The CD player was imprisoned in a cage and was not exactly state of the art but we still sounded polished and edgy. I could see why the album was already gold. The guard had the sound low so people could keep talking, but my mother just wanted to listen, so we didn't talk for a few tracks.

Then came my cover version of "Piece of my Heart." This had been Mr. Goldman's idea. He said every female artist who had a real voice could buy a legion of fans if she nailed this song. Apparently, he was right. To my astonishment, the guard said, "Hey, I know this one," and cranked up the volume. Everyone looked at me.

My mother clutched her chest and wheezed, "Is that really you?"

I'm not sure what drove me—a desire to give her something no one else could give her, some kind of affirmation—but I got to my feet, cleared my throat, and sang to her, patching straight over my own voice track.

She listened with her jaw slack and her hands tightly clasped, and it never crossed my mind that this had to be the most unlikely live performance I would ever give. Instead of silencing me, the guards stood around with their arms folded and their eyes constantly tracking around the room.

Mary wasn't the only one listening. As I rolled out the husky, plaintive notes, I found myself singing to grandmas, small children, faded women and jaded men, the kinds of people who didn't buy CDs and never saw live music. They were completely transfixed, and in that moment it came to me for the first time that I could really sing. That Layla wasn't kidding. I could make an audience eat from my hand.

Admittedly, the term "captive audience" had new meaning in this case, but I was infused with a burst of energy and a confidence I'd never felt before. I felt like the conduit for a power that was not my own, but came from some universal source I'd tapped into. It seemed to connect me to every person in the room and it was as if we fed off one another. I sang louder and gutsier, wanting to reach past the trash life leaves behind to expose the startling beauty hard times obscured.

Long after that day, I would realize how hard it was to do that and how important. It was all too easy to lose sight of what was best and finest in ourselves and in others, and become preoccupied with meaningless trivia.

I had gone to that prison to see where I came from and left seeing where I could go. I felt older. At peace. More at home in myself. And over and over, all the way back to San Francisco, I kept thinking about the last thing my mother said to me.

"Want to know something? I gave birth to you wearing shackles."

CHAPTER FOURTEEN

Here's what happens when you're famous overnight—you go to clubs where the women used to ignore you or they'd dance with you a couple of times then go home with someone else, and all of a sudden, everywhere you look, someone smiles. Every woman you dance with is available and lets you know it. You can't use the bathroom without being propositioned.

I had recently concluded that Suzie was right all along—my animal magnetism was not the drawcard. *I* hadn't changed that much. What *had* changed was that I was the lead singer of Virgin Blessing and the band had performed on *Ellen* last week after the announcement of our Grammy nomination. I could be wearing a puffy shirt, have a bag on my head and talk absolute shit, and I would still be swatting them off like gnats.

I said to Lucrezia, "See her—the one with the white tank and the Celtic tattoo between her shoulders? Last time I was here, she wouldn't dance with me. Now she's like 'wanna come back to my place?'"

"You don't have to settle for her," Luke said. "They're all checking us out."

"Got your eye on anyone?"

"A few." Luke always seemed cool and disinterested, but I'd learned that she chose her target soon after arriving at a venue and would watch her for a while then make a move.

She never went for any of the cute under twenty-fives who hung around hoping to be noticed. She liked women her own age, which was thirty-two; she was the oldest member of the band. Her preferred take-home snack was the kind of woman I always used to wish would hit on me—beautiful, older, smart, and hard to get.

I had studied Luke's pick-up technique, hoping to emulate it. From what I could see, she was fairly subtle, instigating a dance of almost imperceptible cues. I kept thinking I'd try it, but before I could get as far as the repeated eye contact stage, I was saying yes to any woman who came up to me. Through the course of a typical post-performance evening, I would get elegantly wasted, and the next time I saw my role model she'd have the most stunning babe in the room on her arm and be waving good night to me.

Even though I was now deeply sought after as a one-night stand, I still had trouble scoring with a certain kind of woman: specifically, Layla. We saw one another fairly frequently, but always in the context of work. I'd gotten beyond anger, hurt feelings, bewilderment at the ineffectuality of my flower deliveries and dismay over her lukewarm replies to my most heartfelt e-mails. These days, I simply felt mystified.

Something tangible always hovered between us, yet I could not persuade her to have dinner with me. As soon as I started to talk with her on a personal level, she closed me down. I don't know why I kept trying. Just stupid, I guess. Or maybe stubborn. I wasn't even sure what I felt for her anymore. Perhaps my heart wanted to believe hers was the love I was made for. Perhaps, Layla was the one piece of heaven on earth I'd ever known, and like an addict I would eternally chase that first high. Sometimes I thought I was running after a dream. Layla never let me get close enough to separate myth from reality. I'd long ago concluded she wasn't playing hard to get, she simply wasn't interested.

"Want another beer?" Luke asked, compelling me to get a grip on myself.

"No thanks. I might call it a night soon." I felt bored and restless and I'd fucked all the strangers I wanted for one lifetime. It got old, not knowing last names and performing the same sexual script everyone seemed to expect.

I studied Luke covertly. She never seemed to get bored. No doubt the women she attracted were more interesting than the ones I ended up with. I wondered what she had that I didn't have. She was about my height, but she had muscles and a built-in tan from her Native American grandmother. Her hair was dirty blonde and dead straight. She wore it in a ponytail at her nape, tied with a leather thong. Somehow, on her, the look wasn't girly. I realized that was probably because her neck was strong and sinewy and her jaw had a stubborn set. She had light sun-on-grass hazel eyes that seemed even more striking because her eyebrows were very dark. On the rare occasions she smiled, it was a slow, predatory smile that made my heart pound, and *I* didn't even want to sleep with her, at least not often.

Tonight was one of those nights when I was thinking about it. Luke was looking particularly desirable in a skin tight T-shirt that flaunted her impressive biceps, and black leather pants that sat far enough below the waist that her fantastically toned torso constantly attracted greedy stares. Around her neck she wore a heavy silver and gold twisted chain with a small bone charm on it that had belonged to her Navajo grandmother. She said that sometimes while she was playing her guitar she could feel the old lady's spirit as though she were sitting right behind her.

I glanced down at the firm-fleshed hand resting on her knee. Luke always wore the same thick gold band on her right ring finger. It was engraved in a flowing pattern like waves. These were etched in black enamel. I'd wanted to ask her about it before, but I suspected its history was personal and I didn't want to seem nosy.

But tonight, emboldened by our developing friendship, I said, "I like that ring."

"Me too." Not exactly forthcoming.

"Where'd you get it? I was thinking maybe I could order something similar by the same designer."

Her gaze settled on me, revealing nothing of her thoughts. Leaning closer, so I could hear her above the din, she said near my ear, "It was made for me by the only woman I've ever been willing to kill for."

I caught my breath over this flatly spoken admission. "Who was she?"

As soon as I'd asked, I felt silly. Luke wasn't one for spilling her guts. But she seemed in a mellow mood and didn't close the conversation down the way she usually did when people got personal with her. Luke was an expert at delivering a pleasant but nonnegotiable brush-off. The puff pieces about Virgin Blessing that had choked the media lately described her as our "raunchy but mysterious bassist" and "an intensely private musician who brings a maturity to the band."

Salon gushed that "in person she has a stillness about her that speaks of a reflective intellect and passions that run deep," something I would never be accused of. The very same article claimed I sang "with the raunchy, bare-knuckles grit of Janis Joplin and the eloquent pathos of Annie Lennox," a flattering comparison that proved the guy who wrote the piece knew zero about female artists.

Luke would listen to Peaches gleefully reading these determinations and occasionally roll her eyes. I never had the faintest idea what she really thought about anything, least of all what she thought of me. We'd become friends over the past months, or at least allies. I wasn't sure if that was because we were the two out lesbian members of the band and the others were heterosexual or bi, or whether Luke actually liked me as a person. Sometimes I got the impression she was just putting up with me.

I wasn't sure how I felt about her, either. Mostly I was awestruck. She was a fantastic guitarist, classically trained and amazingly versatile. She also played piano, harmonica, and trumpet like a pro and she could get by on about a half dozen other instruments. When she and Bella jammed together they played jazz and swing like they'd grown up in a New Orleans bar.

For my first few months in the band, I was tongue-tied every time Luke spoke to me. Then we drank margaritas one night after she'd put her number in my cell phone and we loosened up with one another. Since then, she'd been a mentor to me, musically speaking, and as things got crazier, she'd allowed me to occupy a small corner of her world, sitting next to her on planes and buses, drinking with her after hours, trawling for women with her at night spots all over the country. This arrangement worked well for me. I got to console the ones she disappointed each night.

I'd stayed close to Suzie the whole time, but she couldn't tour with us, and it was good to have someone on my side who really understood what it was like to stand on stage and perform. There was nothing more naked and lonely and exhilarating. Luke knew that feeling just as I did.

I contemplated the braided leather bracelet around her left wrist, and wondered how it would feel to love someone so much you would kill for them.

"Her name was Irene." Luke surprised me by answering my unspoken question. "She died three years ago."

I had the good taste not to ask how. I said, "I'm very sorry."

"Me too."

Was there a script for the right thing to say when the love of someone's life is dead? Feeling supremely inadequate, I said, "I guess there are some things you don't get over."

She studied my face, as if weighing an idea, then she cast a desultory look around the club and said, "I'm not in the mood for this tonight. How about you?"

"I'm over it," I said, "Let's go somewhere quiet."

"Want to come back to my place?"

I reminded myself that we were friends and nothing else was going on. She hadn't given me any of her hot looks. "Sounds good."

I'd been to Luke's before with the rest of the band one night when we all got pizza and watched scary movies. She had a house in Oakland, which she'd bought before the prices went through the roof and the poor people had to move out. We drove there in her car, a pristine old white Cadillac with powder blue leather upholstery. When I complimented her on its condition, she told me it had belonged to her grandmother. I was hip to collector's cars now, thanks to Eric, whose passion for his Packard was exceeded only by his dedication to the Standish family business.

It was 2:00 a.m. and there wasn't much traffic around. A veil of fog rose from the ocean and shrouded the Bay Bridge, obscuring the city lights behind us. We drove slowly, our tires making swishing sounds like brooms on wet concrete. I thought Luke might talk about the beloved Irene, but instead she put on a CD and offered me a joint. Tonight's stuff was Humboldt-grown Train Wreck, which always made me introspective and maudlin, so I declined.

"Yeah, I'm not up for it either," she said and hit the volume.

She had a Bose sound system and it struck me that we should have been listening to "Wish You Were Here." I certainly felt like a lost soul swimming in a fish bowl, but Luke, evidently, did not share my brooding ennui. She'd put on a Stones album.

We drove for a few minutes, both singing along to "Sympathy for the Devil," then she startled the crap out of me by turning down the music and saying, "Layla's one of my exes too."

"She wasn't my girlfriend," I said hastily. "We just hooked up for a day or two."

"I was with her for three months."

Consumed with envy, and so curious I couldn't contain myself, I asked, "What went wrong?"

"Everything. You know the syndrome. Great sex with the wrong person, lousy sex with someone you could imagine settling down with."

I laughed like I knew exactly what she meant, and wondered which one it was with Layla.

"She was too high maintenance for me." Luke provided the answer I didn't want to hear. "Nothing was ever simple."

"I can imagine." I fought off an image of Layla with her head thrown back against a downy white pillow and Luke making her cry out. My guts clenched. Had they been in love? Luke hadn't said anything about being willing to kill for Layla. A small flutter of relief loosened the tension in my neck.

"Layla happened after Irene. It was a rebound situation." Luke sounded philosophical.

"I thought I was in love with her," I confessed.

"Everyone does."

"How do you know?"

"She told me, and I saw it happen once or twice." She paused, then glanced at me. "It's pretty obvious that you've had a case for her."

I felt my cheeks growing hotter by the second and was glad we were in the car and it was nighttime, so she wouldn't notice. I thought about Eric warning me off Layla during our tense trip to the San Diego airport. It felt like light years ago now.

"She's a really good songwriter," I said, striving for an impersonal note. Layla's music had, after all, provided our band with two hit singles and far more attention than we deserved. I wished I didn't feel sick to my stomach every time she showed up at our sessions. She only had to look at me and my heart throttled my ribcage. "Were you in love with her?" I dared.

Luke frowned and pondered briefly. "No. I felt…consumed by her. It was like vanishing. I think maybe I needed that at the time, but after a while it got uncomfortable."

I stared at her, unable to conceive of anyone with such a forceful presence being able to vanish, let alone wanting to. She glanced sideways and met my eyes before returning her attention to the road ahead. We were heading into Piedmont, not far from her house. I started having second thoughts. What was I doing going home with her in the middle of the night? Why had she invited me?

We stopped at an intersection and I half-turned in my seat and said, "Luke, why are we going back to your place?"

She was silent for a beat. "I don't feel like being alone."

"But you could have had anyone you wanted from that place."

"Precisely." Her eyes drew mine and for once, there was an expression in them I could read. Even with the erratic play of shadows and light from the streetlamps and the traffic signals, I could see candid invitation. "I didn't feel like being with a stranger."

I faced her squarely. "You want to sleep with me?"

"I do, yes."

"As in sex?"

She took my hand and lifted it to her cheek. "We could explore that."

"This feels kind of weird."

"I know." The lights changed and she ignored the signal. We were the only car in our lane. "I can take you home if you want. Just say the word."

I thought about crawling alone into my bed, the known and the safe, and then I thought about lying naked with Luke, the completely unknown and probably dangerous, the kind of woman I never slept with and a fellow band member. We had an unspoken rule about that. Relationships within a band were never a good idea. But my hand tingled beneath hers and I couldn't help but shiver thinking about our bodies in full contact, hers hard against mine.

My stomach nose-dived and I croaked, "Okay. Let's explore."

She turned her face into my palm and planted a kiss there. The lights changed again and, placing my hand on her thigh, she drove. The feel of her muscles through the sensual second skin of leather was strangely transfixing. I moved my hand experimentally and felt a small shock ripple through her body. She caught her breath and I saw what I'd never seen before, a flash of desire that narrowed her eyes and curved her mouth. It changed everything. Time slowly dripped like treacle.

The air seemed heavy and too thick to breathe.

She looked at me again and the simmering promise in her stare got me so wet I shifted traitorously in my seat.

With a husky laugh, she said, "Me too."

My mouth went dry. Knowing that she knew I was getting aroused made me even hotter. All of a sudden all I could think about was sex. I was stunned that I'd never felt this way about her before, that it had snuck up on me so swiftly. I'd had vague speculative thoughts about sleeping with her—in fact, the occasional torrid fantasy. But she was my friend and I knew where my boundaries were. Also, I'd assumed that lusting after her was pointless. She could have anyone. I was sure I would never be in the running.

We drove up a steep hill in Piedmont and made a left into her driveway. The garage door before us opened. She parked inside and I glanced behind me, staring out into the night as the door rolled down on my escape route.

"Do you want to change your mind?" she asked.

I shook my head and climbed out of the car. My legs quivered and I had to bite down on my lower lip to stop it trembling. Luke said something polite and waited for me to join her before walking up the concrete steps to the door that connected the garage to the house. She ushered me ahead of her and flicked on the lights. A dainty white cat was waiting in the tiled hallway. Immediately she wound herself around Luke's legs.

"Meet Blanche," Luke said. "I think she was in hiding last time you were here."

Trying to seem at ease, I crouched and stroked the cat, who stared up at me with one bright blue eye and one green. I scratched around her chin and she purred discreetly. I was more of a dog person, but I could see how cats could fascinate. They only respond to your mawkish overtures if they consider you worthy.

Luke lifted Blanche into her arms and cradled her on her back, kissing her belly and crooning to her. Blanche endured this humiliating ritual with an air of resignation, occasionally casting her odd-eyed stare my way as if to warn me against mirth. I held back, allowing myself to appreciate the softness I could see in Luke. It made her calm strength that much more appealing.

We walked into her living room and she set Blanche on the floor, asking me, "Drink?"

"I've had enough, thanks."

She gave me a knowing look but her face was otherwise inscrutable. "Then we can sit here feeling a bit awkward for a while, or we can go to my room. Your choice."

"Do you feel awkward?"

"Slightly. You're not a stranger."

I could relate. "Weird, huh? It's almost…easier with a stranger."

"It's definitely easier."

"I wonder why." I was genuinely puzzled. Surely knowing one another would lessen the inhibitions when you got naked together. But I felt incredibly tense and queasy, and almost jumped out of my skin when Luke tucked her finger over the belt of my jeans and tugged me toward her.

"Stop thinking about it," she said and lowered her mouth to mine.

Once I'd gotten past the first nervous thrill, I relaxed and let her dictate the pace and intensity of our kiss. She was an expert. Her tongue engaged with mine and she forced my mouth wider, tasting and sucking and softly devouring until I was clinging to her so I wouldn't sink to the floor. I loved the hungry but controlled way she kissed. No one ever kissed me like that, like I was all they wanted.

She took my hips in her hands and backed me into an unlit room, her mouth still stealing the breath from me. Caught by surprise, I didn't even try to see where we were going. She was stronger than me and effortlessly pushed me against a wall, parting my thighs with a knee, her hands releasing my hips to seize my wrists. She pinned my hands lightly above my head, bringing our bodies into full, hard contact.

In my ear, she murmured, "Tell me if you want this to stop."

I was so incredibly wet, my jeans seemed glued to my crotch. The bump in the seam ground against my clit as she worked her knee slowly back and forth. I pushed down, increasing the pressure. "No," I whispered.

Immediately she lowered my hands to my sides and eased back. In the light from the room beyond, I could read the desire in her eyes and something else. Her expression was tender and assessing all at once.

"No, meaning *stop*? Or no—as in, you want this?"

My mouth was so swollen from her kisses, and my throat so dry, I had trouble forming the words. "I want this."

Her hands tightened around mine. "I'm basically a top. Does that work for you?"

It was hard to concentrate on the question with her nipples grazing my chest through the barrier of our clothing and her body heating mine. I tried to frame an honest answer but I wasn't sure what she was really asking and I preferred not to put myself in a box. Everyone was an individual, after all, and I generally played it by ear with my girlfriends. I tried to figure out what women wanted so I could give it to them.

"I'm versatile," I said for lack of a better way to explain this perspective.

"Okay." She lifted my hands and kissed them one at a time. "If you don't feel comfortable at any stage, just tell me."

I wasn't comfortable now. I wanted us to stop talking and start taking off our clothes before I had second thoughts about sleeping with a band member. "I'm cool," I said.

Relinquishing my hands, she cupped my face and kissed me with such passionate precision I thought I would pass out. "Then let go," she murmured against my mouth. "Don't try to control what happens. Just feel."

I thought I was doing that already. "Okay."

She had my belt undone and my jeans open before I could think about whether I really was ready to be naked. "I'm going to fuck you till you can't come anymore," she said and slid her hand inside my panties and along the hot aching furrow of my sex.

She didn't tease or dabble. She cupped me in her hand and squeezed hard, sending a shock of sensation through my body that made me slump forward, resting my weight on her, whining softly. She rocked me on her hand, at the same time kissing and biting my neck. When her fingers finally parted me, I couldn't stop myself from crying out. Almost as the sound was wrenched from me, she thrust inside, opening me faster than anyone ever had.

"Baby, you feel good," she groaned. "I don't know why I waited so long."

"Me either." I wanted our clothes off. I wanted to feel her skin against mine. Yet I could concentrate on nothing but the fierce, fast rhythm of her stokes, the cigar-and-leather scent of her, the need to breathe or pass out. I tilted my pelvis, improving on her entry angle. Her other hand found my ass, lifting me to her, making me take her deeper. We converged and grunted and clung together, urging each other on. She fucked me harder and faster until I was just moments away from coming, my muscles straining, my breath ragged, harsh little whines rising from my throat. Then, suddenly, I was empty and her wet hand brushed over my belly.

A shock of panic and craving engulfed me. "Don't stop," I gasped out. "Why did you stop?"

She laughed softly and hustled me toward the bed a few feet away. "I'm not stopping. In fact"—she shoved me down against the pillows and roughly pulled off my jeans and panties—"I haven't even started."

Far above me, through a broad skylight, stars crowded a serenely radiant moon, but I soon relinquished the draw of the celestial for the immediacy of the woman I was with. She helped me out of my shirt and we both stared down at my body, pale in the watery glow of the moonlight. I had goose flesh, not just because I was naked and the room was a little cool, but the way she looked at me made me shiver and pulse with anticipation.

I reached for her, needing her inside me once more, but she stepped just out of reach and into the shadows. I squirmed as I waited for what seemed an eternity. I could hear drawers opening and closing, clothing being discarded, muted sounds I didn't recognize. Frustrated and bent on relief, I slid my hand down to my welling core. I had barely made contact when she caught my wrist.

"Did I say you could touch yourself?"

I looked up at her and a tremor passed through me. She hadn't undressed and was standing next to the bed in her leather pants and a plain white T-shirt.

"Would you like to watch?" I offered.

"I'll let you know if you can please me that way." She released my hand and bent down to kiss my cheek.

At the same time she clamped one of my nipples between two fingers and squeezed until pain and pleasure combusted into a single intense sensation that was neither. It went straight to my groin and my insides clenched a response that made me cry, "Luke, please."

"All in good time."

She caught the other nipple, adding to my desperation. Her breath caressed my cheek, then her mouth moved over my throat and down to the nipple she'd chosen first. With the tip of her tongue she took over from her fingers and massaged the sensitized flesh, kissing and blowing and making me want that exquisite pressure again, and more. When I could bear her tantalizing play no longer, I clutched hold of her, pushing down on her shoulders, urging her to go lower. I parted my thighs and lifted my hips.

She answered, but not the way I expected. Her mouth still busy, she reached behind her and took something from her clothing. Two small metallic clips dangled from a slender chain.

Disconcerted, I said, "I've never used those before."

She knelt over me, straddling one of my thighs. "Well, that's a pity"—she slid the first clamp over my right nipple and deftly fastened it—"because I have a feeling you'll enjoy them. Also, I like to work hands free."

I watched with startled fascination as she slid a bar up the two sides of the clip until my nipple was compressed just enough to make me moan. I wanted to watch her fasten the second one but my concentration kept slipping to the feel of her knee, encased in warm leather and positioned between my thighs, barely skimming my clit. I shimmied down the bed and almost came in sheer relief as I brought myself fully in contact with her.

Luke allowed me to roll my hips back and forth as she finished tightening the second clamp. Then her hands slid beneath my thighs and she pushed me back up the bed and kept pushing until my legs were splayed wide, the knees out to each side, exposing me completely.

"Don't move," she said and got off the bed.

She lit a candle and placed it on a dresser against the opposite wall, then returned to the bed, where she leaned casually against the decorative footboard post to my left. She stared down at me, and I felt shockingly naked knowing that the soft light beamed directly between my thighs, presenting her with an unobstructed view.

"Now you can play with yourself," she said and slid a hand slowly back and forth over the snap front fly of her pants and down toward the recess of her groin.

Uncertainly, I touched myself and caught the flash of a smile.

"That's right. Part yourself for me." When I hesitated, she said huskily, "You're beautiful, baby. I want to watch you come. Will you do that for me?"

There was something quite hypnotic about her calm voice and steady gaze, and the motion of her hand as she aroused herself. The mild steady pressure of the clamps on my nipples also factored in. If I didn't come soon I would combust. Much as I wanted her to deliver my first orgasm, I also wanted to see her turned on and losing control. I wanted to tease her the way she was teasing me.

With one hand I fanned myself apart, and with the other I dipped a couple of fingers deep inside and slowly withdrew, pulling a web of fluids with me. I met her gaze and said, "Look how wet you've made me." Taking my time, I licked my fingers clean before moving them to my clit.

Eyes closed, I followed the familiar route to release I'd taken again and again fantasizing about women I knew and didn't know, about faceless strangers and lovers long lost and yet to be. I could remember none of them now. All I saw, in my mind's eye, was Luke, standing at the end of the bed, arousing herself as she watched me. My fingers did their work, circling and caressing the stiff knot of my clit, stretching and flicking and tugging until I was lost in pleasure. My back arched of its own accord and I lowered my feet, digging my heels into the bed, pushing against my hand. Tension built, my womb cramped, my breathing grew rapid and shallow.

I knew the noises I could hear were my own incoherent cries, and the wet kiss of my fingers appeasing that uncontrollable itch. But something else tickled my senses and I became aware of the hushed language of leather flexing over skin. Then she was there, right next to me, her weight changing the way the mattress supported my feet, making me roll slightly onto one side.

I forced my eyes open and brought her face into focus, just inches from mine. Her gaze locked with mine and she ran her finger gently along the slender chain that connected my nipples and gave a small tug. A flurry of pleasure careened along my nerves and converged at my center. I gasped, "Oh, God."

"Come on, baby. Let it go." Her mouth parted mine and she murmured hot, sweet words as I gulped for air and strained for release, writhing and whimpering and thrusting my hips faster.

My blood thundered in my ears and a thin keening cry rose from my throat. I could only sob as I gave in to one powerful contraction after another. Luke lifted me into her arms and held me as the twitching abated and my panting slowed. All the while she stroked me and tended to me, smoothing my hair, wiping my face, telling me how perfect I was. Eventually, when my breathing slowed, she eased away and passed me a bottle of water from the night table.

I drank slowly so I didn't choke, then handed the bottle back to her and flopped against the pillows, unable to stop smiling. Staring up at the stars, I demanded, "Now, will you fuck me?"

Her eyes glinted. "Yes, baby. But first…" She touched the nipple clamp nearest her. "I think these have done their job and since you're a clamp virgin, I don't want you wearing them for too long."

Warning me that I would feel some pain, she gradually lowered the slide on each. I flinched as the circulation rushed to my nipples. Tenderly she took them one at a time in her mouth, warming and soothing. I wallowed in the sight, overwhelmed with a flood of emotion. A second wave of yearning encompassed me and I ran my hand over her strong shoulders and down her back, loving the shift and squeeze of her muscles.

She lifted her head and straightened, kneeling but resting back on her heels. I made my way upright and knelt to face her. Beneath the thin white cotton of her T-shirt, her nipples rose to greet me. I lifted my hands to them, allowing them to push against my palms. She caught her breath and changed position, rising off her heels to draw me close. Our bodies aligned, hers pressing to mine, and I felt for the first time a distinctive bulge at her crotch. I looked down and ran my hand lightly over the outline of a cock sheathed beneath the leather. Belatedly shy, I backed up.

I didn't have a lot of experience playing with toys. Some partners had wanted me to strap it on and I did, but I always felt inept and on some level dismayed by their enthusiasm for the fake phallus.

Over the years, I'd put up with reeducation from Suzie about my yesterday attitude and my discomfort over terminology, choice of toy shape, appearance, and all the rest. It had taken me a while to recognize that toys were not about wanting men, or pretending to be men, or not being a real lesbian. We had the power and the right to give and receive pleasure any way we chose.

Luke liked to fuck her partners with a toy. Who was I to make that wrong? Anyway, I would be lying if I said I wasn't turned on by the idea. I wanted her inside of me again and I was past caring about the technicalities.

She took my hand in hers and placed it firmly over the accessory in question. "It's not essential, but I know how to use it and I think you'll be happy."

I decided not to pretend sophistication I didn't have. My cheeks felt red and my voice was hoarse. "I don't have a lot of experience with, er…"

She silenced me with a kiss. "It's not important. I have plenty."

Her mouth moved hotly down my throat and shoulder and her hands took possession of my body, caressing and stroking until I could no longer think clearly. Somehow, she sensed exactly when my mind closed down and my body took over.

She sat me back against the pillows, and got off the bed. Standing at the side closest to me, she drew off her T-shirt and tossed it to the floor. Her breasts were not full, but were fleshy and sat high on her chest, the nipples dark and hard.

"Undo me," she said. "See what I have for you."

I was getting wetter by the moment. My fingers fumbled with the metal snaps that kept her cock confined beneath the straining leather. I tilted my head slightly and found her gazing at me with such intensity that I started shaking and quickly looked down again, knowing what was coming. I was so transfixed, then, that I had to force my eyes off the dark, thick shape that emerged from her pants; there was so much more of her to enjoy.

Luke was maybe an inch taller than me, but we didn't have much in common physically. She carried no surplus and was toned all over. Her shoulders and biceps were smooth and hard, her abs chiseled, her thighs powerful. She wasn't a bodybuilder; she was more graceful than that. I reached out and dragged a fingertip over her belly and down onto her jutting cock. A frisson of alarm arrested my breathing. How would I take all that?

"Relax," she said, because apparently I was pitifully transparent to the people I most wanted to impress. "It'll be just fine. In fact, I'm going to let you control this."

I moved over to make room as she sat down on the bed. She swung her legs up and leaned back against the headboard, tucking a few pillows behind her back. "Get on me," she invited.

Soaked and swollen, I happily swung one leg over and sank down onto her lap. I could feel her cock lengthwise beneath me, trapped between her thighs. Experimentally, I rubbed back and forth. A salty sweet leather smell invaded my nostrils. She'd left her pants on and was adjusting them so I could feel the firm texture of her harness.

Desire winnowed the strength from my limbs and my head drooped onto her shoulder. "I want you so much," I said shakily.

Smiling, she slid one arm around me and lifted me off her just enough to move her other hand between my legs. Her fingers worked my opening, dipping, stretching, and circling while her thumb massaged my clit. She slid two fingers inside and curled them hard, heading straight for my G-spot. At the same time she depressed her thumb to sandwich my flesh in a thrilling vice that made me writhe with need.

"Well, I don't think we need any lube," she said.

"Don't make me wait anymore," I gasped. "I can't stand it."

She shifted fractionally beneath me and withdrew her fingers. Before a protest could form in my throat, I felt the head of her cock at my entrance and her hand guiding it into position.

We stared at one another in a moment of fraught anticipation. I could not take my eyes off her face, seeing in the half-lit haze of candle and moon what I'd never seen in her before—a vulnerability she hid from the world. In her desire, she was just as exposed as I was, just as much a lonely creature seeking a mate. We both recognized it—I could tell by the way her lips parted on a fractured breath. In that same stark instant, I saw something else—a wild joy that cast all else into shadow...past loves and sorrows, confusion and expectations, foolish mistakes and blind obsessions. I felt it too, and all I knew was that I was here, whole and complete, with her. I bent and kissed her and for several noisy heartbeats, we trembled against one another in the shared sanctuary of tenderness.

"I love you, Luke." The words fell out, startling me because they were true. I did love her.

It wasn't the frantic infatuation I'd felt for a few women, but something calmer and more profound. We spent so much time together,

I was astounded that I'd never been aware of this before. I truly liked her. I could be myself with her. We trusted each other.

"I love you too, Chance," she said huskily.

We smiled at one another, then something raw passed between us and her eyes narrowed and glittered with lust. Her smile changed to a wolfish grin and her hands moved over my hips. She lifted her pelvis, teasing my folds with her cock just enough to make me squirm.

I rocked my hips, wanting more and trying to slide down on her. But she held me immobile as she teased. "Please," I finally pleaded, "Now, Luke."

Her response was immediate. With a ragged gasp, she pulled me down on her, filling me completely. I yelped in shock. She went in so deep, I could feel the head of her against my cervix. I was afraid to move in case she went any farther, but I couldn't stay still either. I grabbed her shoulders and eased myself up onto my knees, almost displacing the full length of her. Poised above the rounded head, I said, "I thought I was meant to have control of this."

She gave a languid half-smile. "Go ahead. Take control."

I slid gradually down, giving myself the chance to adjust to the girth, at least that was the theory. The truth was, the thrill of feeling her slowly sinking into me, of my walls being pried apart, made me want the sensation over and over. I indulged myself, gradually building the tempo until I became aware once more of that familiar imperative. I had to come. I'd waited long enough. I leaned forward and grasped the headboard posts on either side of her, bearing down faster and faster.

Her fingers dug into me, her mouth found one of my nipples. Sweat ran down my back. Everywhere our skin connected, it sucked and slithered. I felt dizzy, hardly able to stay upright, but intent on the sensual eruption building within. I was caught by surprise and almost burst into tears when she lifted me off her between strokes and threw me onto my back.

"Two seconds"—she placed a finger against my lips—"and I'll take care of you."

She shed the last of her clothes and advanced across the bed to me. Roughly, she kneed my legs apart and settled her weight between them. "Open wide," she said, and slammed into me, smooth and hot.

Instinctively, I clung to her, my legs wrapped around her waist, my arms holding her upper body mashed to mine. She fucked me like she couldn't trust there'd ever be another time, pumping into me, demanding I take all of her, lifting my legs so she could bury herself harder and faster. At times I could only lie back with my eyes closed, in full surrender, hers to use. At other times I watched her face, the eyes dark with avid concentration, the jaw set, sweat gluing her hair to her forehead

We fucked and rocked and groaned together until I was sobbing out little cries and repeating her name over and over. I'd held off my orgasm for as long as I could because I wanted to keep going. I wanted her to come with me, in me. I could feel myself right on the brink, my skin burning, my heart racing. I clamped down on her and held fast, blood rushing in my ears.

She held me to her and kissed me between cries and grunts. "Baby, come. Do it for me," she moaned, reducing me to a weak, wet, writhing thing solely preoccupied with the place where our bodies were joined.

I couldn't even thrust back anymore. I just let go and accepted what she gave me, convulsing when she withdrew almost completely and stared down, seeking my cue.

"Now," I managed and she drove back into me and stayed there for the contractions that pulsed from my core into my belly. Each seemed stronger and more sustained than the last, storming through my body, erasing the woman I had been and replacing her with one who knew more. Shaking and sobbing, I could not will a single movement from my limbs. Everything was involuntary. I felt her fingers in my hair, her cheek against mine, her heart frantically pounding the walls of my chest.

"Stay," I said, as she started to withdraw. I couldn't bear to lose her yet.

A long while later, we unlocked, drank water, and basked. She unfastened her harness and we fumbled our way beneath the bedcovers. She took me in her arms and we kissed slowly and deeply.

"Go to sleep," she said.

"But what about you?"

"Perhaps that can be your first job in the morning."

It didn't sound like an order, so I boldly drew the sheet down to expose her breasts. I was exhausted but wildly elated too. And I wanted to make love to her.

She laughed and her palms settled on my head. "Well, if you insist." Twisting her fingers in my hair, she guided me down.

My mouth shook as I inhaled her scent and took my first tentative taste. I wanted to do this perfectly. I wanted to give as generously to her as she had to me. For the first time in my life, I felt like I was with someone I could truly please. I never knew how much I'd needed that until I took her in my mouth and heard her sigh my name.

CHAPTER FIFTEEN

Here we were, lying side by side long after the afterglow. This was common-sense time—early in the morning, the time when sensible people acknowledge that in the heat of the moment, you say things to each other you don't really mean and read more into such declarations than you should.

I had told Luke I loved her. I glanced sideways at her profile and realized nothing had changed. I still felt the same.

She must have felt me looking, because she turned her head and said, "Just so you can stop with the post mortem and self-torture, I still love you."

I let myself enjoy that simple but heart-stopping declaration, then said, "I hate how you always know what I'm thinking."

"You have an open face."

Instinctively, I tried to freeze my expression as if she might see how soppy I suddenly felt that I was here with her and we weren't being all morning-after distant with each other. Instead we were at ease. Friends. Only closer, all of a sudden.

Impulsively, I asked, "How did you become...you? You the person, I mean. The way you are." I was not explaining my question very well. What I should have said is: cool, smart, talented, effortlessly hot, always the voice of reason, completely together, and an incredibly gifted lover. But that would have sounded gushy.

She shrugged. "I stopped trying to be someone else."

I pondered on this. "Just before my last birthday I decided to change myself."

"Why?"

"I felt...dull. I wasn't really living life. It was like I was just passing time, waiting for something—or some*one*—to happen to me. Have you ever felt like that?"

"I think everyone feels that some time."

"My friend Suzie—the one with the red pigtails—" I thought about my birthday party. I'd spent all evening worrying that they would go home together after Luke got back from having Siren's boyfriend arrested. For some reason, it killed me to think of her and my best friend getting it on. I understood this anxiety better now.

"I know Suzie." Luke turned onto her side to face me, smiling indulgently, as she often did when I was rambling. "What about her?"

"Suzie says our culture defines love too rigidly. She says she and I have a romantic friendship. We're passionate about one another but it's platonic. I was trying to figure out what she'd say about you and me."

"That we're hot together and we should make the most of it," Luke suggested.

I grinned. "What about the rules? No involvement with other band members."

"They'll have to cope." She moved across the bed and leaned over me, her bright hazel eyes roaming my face. "You know what I'd like... I'd like to be your lover. The only one."

I felt like a goldfish, my mouth opening and closing as I circled back and forth around her words.

"Last night...for me. It was kind of unexpected," she said. "Not the sex—I decided a while ago that we were going there."

"You did?" News to me.

"I was waiting for you to get beyond Layla," she said in a matter-of-fact way.

Was I beyond Layla? I called to mind, as I often did, that moment in her arms when I felt blissfully at home. An odd sadness engulfed me. It seemed so long ago that it almost felt unreal, like a long-held wish that only briefly came true. All I had was the memory. The wish had lost its power. I had moved on. I realized that whatever might have been between me and Layla had passed us by. I had not met her amidst depravity and loud music—that should have told me something. But Luke, on the other hand...

"You might have given me a clue," I said.

"I wanted to be your friend first. I was trying something different."

I blushed. The thought that Luke had me in her crosshairs all this time made me giddy.

"In the past, most of my relationships have started with sex and ended with tears," she said with mild irony. "They say if you want a different outcome you can't keep doing the same thing. So…here we are."

I tucked my hand into hers. "Do you think it's okay that we're not in love?"

"I've stopped thinking love comes prepackaged," she said. "The thing is, I can see myself falling in love with you and I'd like to let it happen."

I'd never thought about love that way. I thought it just happened and there was no way to control it. You certainly couldn't *make it* happen; I knew that much from trying to be in love with women who were nice to me. But that wasn't what Luke was suggesting. I understood exactly what she meant.

"I think, if I let myself, I would be in love with you too." I found my way into her arms. "I have to tell you…last night was a good start."

She grinned and I ran my fingers over the defined planes and curves of her face. I hadn't noticed before how finely shaped her mouth was, broad and firmly etched with a slight cleft in the lower lip. The tiny smile lines at each corner hinted at her dry sense of humor. She had a strong chin and jaw that balanced her high cheekbones. I suspected these were another legacy from her grandmother.

In the early morning sunlight, her eyes were light amber with flecks of jade. The lashes were dark and dead straight. She had an interesting face, a face I would want to sculpt if I knew how.

"Do we have to go to work?" I murmured.

She traced a finger over my lips and down to the cleft she'd left sore just hours earlier. "I guess we could show up late."

I grinned and stretched languidly in her arms. "So, make me stay."

❖

Grace Lennox

Once the buzz died down after the Grammy nomination, Mr. Goldman hired a new publicist for us. He said we needed to keep the momentum going right up to the awards ceremony. Tiggy Marshall was a Machiavellian mistress of the music industry celeb factory—just what we needed if we were going to bag the award and move to "the next level."

Tiggy was maybe fifty, but surgically youthed down to forty, and drank her Ketel One martinis extra dry and dirty with two olives. She wore black everything and a pair of Clark Kent glasses with black plastic frames. Her mouth was bee stung from regular collagen and very dark crimson to match her nails, which were surprisingly short for a woman who had made an art form of muckraking. These days, Tiggy was hired to stage-manage the very same people she'd once character-assassinated in the tabloids. Now her specialty was turning publicity-seekers without talent, class, or noble virtues into front page news in *People* and *Us*.

I was not sure whether we should be insulted or flattered that Mr. Goldman had hired this big gun to take charge of our image.

"Let's face it, ladies," Tiggy announced in a high-pitched nasal twang that made me want to take drugs. "If fuck knows *how* many flacks could do it for Paris Hilton, I can do it for you."

"But none of us has that revolving man-door thing going on," Luke said after a contemplative puff on her cigar. I could hardly look at her and sit straight. I wanted her relentlessly. I felt like someone in a cult, programmed to emit copious quantities of fluid every time my girlfriend spoke.

Tiggy responded with an intensity of concentration that made her lips compress, but did not budge her Botoxed brow by one iota. "Okay"—her small, round blue eyes swept us—"hands up, the girls into girls."

Luke and I lifted a paw each, acknowledging the lesbo mindset but refraining from looking at one another in case we inadvertently advertised our passion. Normally we kept a lid on things by making out in bathrooms, dressing rooms, green rooms, and hotel rooms all over the country when we thought no one would notice us missing at the same time.

"It depends." Peaches toyed with her pink extensions. She was an indecisive type of person, and this extended to her love life. She said she didn't know if she was really bisexual—she couldn't make up her

• 192 •

mind about that.

"From now on you are all heterosexual but hip," Tiggy instructed. "Which means you can be lesbian-friendly, you can even do girl-on-girl so long as you describe it to journalists as fun experimentation. But publicly, men are your arm candy."

"Well, I asked Billie Joe Armstrong," Peaches interjected with saccharine irony, "but he's, like…married with kids."

Siren, also a Billie Joe admirer and now single, said, "Have you seen his wife?"

"Gorgeous," Peaches griped. "And it sounds like it's true love. Can you believe it? All that, and happy too." She heaved a resigned sigh and placed her hand on Tiggy's knee. "I guess it'll just have to be you and me, Ms. Marshall."

Tiggy laughed like a hyena and relocated the hand back onto Peaches's lap. "I've compiled a list of available male rockers and actors," she informed us. "If anyone has a personal preference, I'll take that on board, otherwise I'll just go ahead and set up opportunities."

I felt extremely dull-witted. "Opportunities for what?"

"Photographs." She slowed down a little and, as if addressing the special class, pasted on a patronizing smile and instructed, "Each of you will appear at events and venues where the target male is present. You will be introduced to him. Smile big like he's your boyfriend. Get his arm around you. Most males do it instinctively. I want you up close and personal. A kiss on the cheek works. We need the suggestion of intimacy."

"Oh, Christ," Luke said.

"But won't these males be surprised?" I pictured a startled movie star wondering why I was acting like his lover.

Tiggy brushed this aside like I'd lost my mind. "No, they expect females to be all over them. Remember, you're not just fans, you're new celebrities. Everyone knows the score."

"The score?" Luke looked like she could hardly wait to leave.

"It's all about publicity. For you. For them. It's a win/win."

"Girl, are you crazy?" Bella interjected. "My mama will fry my ass if she sees me hitting on white boys. And Daddy…I don't even want to go there."

Unfazed, Tiggy rifled through a notebook. "I thought that might be an issue, so I've made a short list of fine, proud African American men any parents would welcome into their home."

"Oh, you have?" Bella rarely showed annoyance, but she put her hands on her hips and swung her head back, her chin jutting out.

The last time I'd seen her do this was when we were watching CNN with the sound down while we waited for our recording studio to clear out. A hip-hop kid attached to the act ahead of us saw Rosa Parks's picture on the screen and asked who she was. I thought Bella was going to thump him.

Tiggy wasn't done with us. "Next year, after you've won a Grammy, we'll need an autobiography from your lead singer and we'll do a book about the band."

"I'm only twenty-eight," I said, trying to imagine how I could dredge up enough self-aggrandizing anecdotes to fill two hundred pages. "Don't you need to have had a life and achieved something before you write a book?"

"No, you only have to be rich and desperate for attention," Luke said.

Tiggy removed her eye fashion like it pained her to have to see me in focus. "It's unwise to wait until your celebrity curve is a flatliner," she warned. "Don't worry, you won't even have to read it."

I started laughing and it set everyone else off.

"We're going to break the ice with a *Vanity Fair* piece on your songwriter," Tiggy continued.

"Me? In *Vanity Fair*?" Peaches squealed. "Fierceness! You're as good as Nicole Richie's publicist!"

"Who's Nicole Richie?" I asked. The name seemed familiar but I couldn't remember anything about the woman.

"Nobody," Tiggy said. "But you've heard of her and that's thanks to someone like me." She consulted her BlackBerry. "Layla Wilde is your songwriter, isn't she?"

Peaches froze. She looked so deflated I wanted to slap this hired sycophant.

"Layla's written some of our material," Luke said coldly. "But Peaches formulated the concept for our first album. It's her writing that has defined the band."

"Okay, so that's another piece." Tiggy made notes with a little plastic pencil. "Excellent. I'm going to send Harold over to interview you on the creative make-up of the band, the personalities, your history. Harold is my assistant and a fine journalist. He worked spin for the

White House, then he was with BNC—Jessica Simpson's people—before I headhunted him."

This was a recommendation? I said, "Great, let's get indicted. That'll make an *E! News* headline."

Tiggy looked like she actually gave this idea some room, but she was back on track in short order. "What was I saying? Oh yes, *Vanity Fair*. This is a prestige piece for us. As I'm sure you all know, Ms. Wilde is a cousin of Eric Standish, the wealthy bachelor who appeared on the cover of GQ last month. Mr. Standish is rumored to be dating Chelsea Clinton, so we have a major news item tie-in." She turned her ruthless gaze on me. "I understand you're a personal friend of Mr. Standish's."

It was stupid, but I just wanted to prove that Tiggy Marshal didn't know *everything*, so I said, like it was old news, "We were engaged for a while."

My enjoyment at seeing her jaw drop was tempered by a sharp look from Luke. I had never told her about my embarrassing fake engagement. It was history and not important to us. What I had told her, however, was that I'd never been with a man. She liked that.

"You were engaged?" Peaches was wide-eyed. "I thought you totally shopped in the girl department."

"Paydirt," Tiggy breathed. "A former fiancée. That's made in heaven. We'll have you all over the newsstands once the gossip breaks about him and Chelsea."

"I think you'll find there's no basis to that rumor," I said.

"It doesn't matter." She was moving right along. "We're not in the truth business. Leave that to the *New York Times*."

To Luke, I half-whispered, "It's not like you think. He's queer."

She gave me one of her slow, smoldering smiles and startled everyone by stubbing out her cigar and coming over to stand behind my chair. Bending down so her mouth was right next to my ear, she said quietly, "If you keep secrets from me, I'll have to punish you."

I tilted my head as if I were listening intently, when really I was just trying to brush my lips across her cheek. "You know everything worth knowing about me, darling."

Siren groaned. "Get a room, you two."

I didn't think we were *that* obvious. "We're just friends," I said innocently.

At which point, Bella cracked up, lowering her head and laughing so hard her beaded braids clattered.

Peaches, also clutching herself, hiccupped, "You should see your face. You're pinker than my hair."

Luke caressed my shoulder. "Okay, ladies. You're embarrassing my girlfriend. Let's move on."

I covered her hand with my own and beamed up at her, happy that she'd finally broken it to the group. We'd been talking about the timing for the past three months, ever since we got together, but we'd agreed to wait and see how things went before we made any big announcements. How things had gone was that we were now talking about moving in together. Suzie was the only person I'd told and she was completely enamored of Luke, telling me all the time that I was the luckiest woman alive and we should just get married and have babies.

I wasn't ready for that, but I could see myself living with Luke— we almost did, already. We were very compatible in the home and garden sense, as well as in every other department. I could not imagine how I'd ever thought I could belong with anyone else.

Tiggy surveyed us impatiently. She didn't seem bothered that Luke and I were an item, only that we should be discreet about it. "Don't be seen together in Bed, Bath & Beyond," she told us.

"Congratulations, by the way," Bella said. "You two are made for each other."

Everyone kissed us and Peaches said, "We should have a party! We don't have to tell anyone what we're really celebrating. It could be because we've gone platinum."

Tiggy cast an approving glance at her. "Good thinking. I'll get busy on a guest list."

I pushed one of Suzie's cards into her hand and said, "This is the woman we hire to cater band functions. She's also my best friend."

"Then she's hired." Tiggy pocketed the card. "One last thing." She lowered her tone to an ominous mezzo-soprano. "Never, I repeat...*never*, speak to the police or the media before you talk to me. It doesn't matter what's going down. You're shitfaced and you flatten some homeless guy, you're busted, you catch your husband or whatever fucking your best friend and blow their brains out. Call me. Do you understand?"

We all nodded. Mr. Goldman had given similar instructions.

"And the other thing. Everyone has secrets. Everyone has a past. If there's anything that could damage the band, I need to know about it. A preemptive strike is the key to damage control. That's what I've done with Ms. Wilde's story."

Queasily, I asked, "What is Ms. Wilde's story?"

Tiggy looked as contented as an ax murderer wiping off a blade. "You'll just have to read about it."

❖

"Christ," Luke said.

We had the Gutenberg bible of starfucking spread flat on the table between us, and in classic *Vanity Fair* form, the headline hooked us: THE MURDER-SUICIDE THAT WASN'T: WHAT THE SAN DIEGO ELITE KNOWS BUT ISN'T SAYING ABOUT THE DAISY ROMNEY KILLING .

I started reading but this month's perfume strips were making my eyes water too much. "Did you know about this?"

Luke shook her head. "No way."

There was Layla, a picture taken when she was college age. The caption said: *Layla Wilde, 20, with Brown University roommate and lesbian lover Daisy Romney.* On the same page was a recent shot of Eric, looking like the dashing urban sophisticate he was, and a few small Standish family photographs.

Luke spent the next half hour reading aloud a story so horrible I was crying by the end. Layla had been in love with a girl from another rich San Diego family. They thought no one knew about their relationship, but Daisy's older brother found out. The article speculated that he told their father, Franklin Romney, who was descended from a long line of patrician bigots who didn't want Jews and black people in their country clubs and thought queer was quaint so long as it didn't happen in his family.

One hot July, during the vacation, Mr. and Mrs. Romney went sailing for a long weekend in their monstrous yacht. Daisy didn't go because she wanted to spend time with Layla while her parents were not at home. It was a Saturday night and Daisy's older brother, Mark, was having a party. There were several versions of what went down at the Romney mansion that night but the police and pathologists agreed on certain key facts. Layla was stabbed in a gatehouse and apparently left for dead. Daisy went looking for her, evidently fearful, for she carried a gun. When she found Layla, she shot herself in the head. Police thought the noise must have roused Layla, who was bleeding to death. She managed to drag herself to a phone and call 911.

Layla was found to have had sex with more than one man soon before the incident but claimed to remember nothing about it. According to the story she gave police, she went to the gatehouse to meet Daisy after receiving a note from her. The journalist writing the *VF* article quoted an anonymous source who said several of the young men at the party were told by Daisy's brother that there was a drugged girl in the gatehouse whom they could rape if they wanted. At the time, the participants told the police the sex was consensual and everyone was just drunk and having fun.

Layla and Daisy's relationship was made invisible, despite the fact that it suggested a motive for foul play and made the rape allegations more credible. After the initial investigations were concluded and Daisy's death swept quietly under the carpet as a tragic suicide, Layla's family sent her overseas for the rest of her education.

The case had been reopened recently after Mark Romney's ex-wife made some inflammatory statements during their messy divorce. She claimed Mark threatened her that he had "plenty of practice taking care of females who cause problems to my family." He told her how he'd lured Layla to the gatehouse, drugged her and raped her. He'd then encouraged several of his buddies to do the same so that "there'd be no clear evidence of who was responsible."

The ex–Mrs. Romney was convinced he spoke to his father, then went back and stabbed the girl. Other anonymous sources quoted by *Vanity Fair* also suggested Franklin Romney had ordered his son to kill Layla. The article theorized that Daisy had smelled a rat and followed Mark to the gatehouse, that they'd struggled and he'd forced the gun to her head, making it look like suicide.

In the end, the police were hamstrung in their investigation by a wall of silence as friends, family, and staff of the Romneys closed ranks to protect the family.

"No wonder Layla's...difficult." I tried to imagine living every day wondering if my first love had blown her brains out after thinking I was dead, or if she'd been murdered by members of her own family because of our relationship. "She never told you any of this?"

Luke looked shaken. "Not a word. The whole time we were together, it made me nuts that she never seemed happy, no matter what I did."

"This is an interesting comment." I pointed to one of the final paragraphs.

Layla had agreed to be interviewed for the article and I figured that was why Tiggy was so pleased with herself. The slant of the piece painted Layla as the innocent victim of a terrible crime, a survivor who had paid a huge personal price for her sexuality.

"There is nothing to be gained from dragging this up, now," Layla was quoted as saying, "Daisy is gone, but there are other people I love whose lives I would not choose to place at risk. Franklin and Mark Romney are ruthless men with friends in high places. And we live in a world that allows ruthless men to get away with murder if they are rich and powerful enough."

"We have to do something," I said, wiping my eyes. "She's basically saying she can't tell the truth because she's too terrified."

Was this why Layla could never let herself love anyone? Was she afraid they would become a target? Had she been blackmailed into silence all these years? I could see Luke had drawn the same conclusions.

Her face pale, she lit a cigar and said, "I'm not sure what we *can* do. She's right. These people are a law unto themselves."

I thought about my birth mother, incarcerated because she'd murdered a man in cold blood. Fair enough. But why was Mark Romney walking free?

"It's not right," I said, outraged. "We have to help her."

"Baby, I think Layla is the only person who can decide how to handle this."

"No," I said adamantly. "Some one has to stand up for her. If her family won't, then it will have to be us."

Luke took me in her arms and kissed me with distracting thoroughness. "Count me in, but I want your promise that you'll have her agreement to anything you're planning to do about this."

"I promise." I drew her closer and returned her kiss with all the passion she stirred in me. "I love you," I said, "I waited my whole life for you."

She held me hard against her. "I love you too, baby."

"Would you kill for me?" I half-teased. Every so often I gave her an opening to tell me about Irene, but she never responded.

This time, Luke took my face between her hands and stared into my eyes. "I would die for you."

"Let's hope it doesn't come to that," I said cheekily, and scrambled away from her.

"Come here and say that." Hot menace flooded her voice and she grabbed my ankle.

"Just try and make me."

She dragged me down the bed and pinned me easily with her weight. "What were you saying?"

I stopped wriggling and said, "We're so lucky."

She smiled and kissed me with infinite tenderness. "I want all of you. Always."

"You have me," I said. "I'm yours."

EPILOGUE

So, here I am, writing my biography before I'm thirty. Outrageous. Everyone has a story but I have to tell mine way too soon because Tiggy Marshall says our fans will suck it up.

Like me, you are probably wondering if Layla finds justice in the end. And if I live happily ever after with Luke and if she ever tells me about Irene. You want to know what happens to Suzie and Eric, and whether Reverie ever writes to me, and if I end up going to a Kinky Salon Halloween Party? What about my birth mother? Do I hire a fancy lawyer and fight to have her paroled?

The answer to all the above is, I have no idea. None of it has happened yet, and that's why people should wait until they're sixty before they rush their life history into print.

What I can tell you is that life is full of surprises. The journey can be as safe or as perilous as you want, but it will never be completely predictable. Sometimes things happen that you can't control. Sometimes you fuck up and there are unhappy consequences. But you can have amazing adventures if you're willing to take some risks and learn from your mistakes.

So far, the adventure I recommend most of all is love. It comes in many guises, each of them uniquely beautiful, each expanding the capacity for more. Love isn't easy. You can't buy it at a drive-through. The more you invest in it, the more it is worth and the harder it is to lose. But even doomed love and love-that-might-have-been have something to teach.

Layla and I were talking one day. Actually it was the day we visited Daisy Romney's grave.

"I was crazy for you," I said, choked up and tortured by the past. "I thought we were meant to be together."

"We are, but not as lovers." Layla took my hand and we walked across the springy lawn toward Eric's Packard. "You have no idea how much I needed you in my life right then. I was so close to giving up. But you made me decide to go on."

I was stunned. "What did I do?"

"You reminded me of Daisy. You looked beyond the packaging and you beckoned an inner self I thought was lost forever. After La Jolla, I knew that I could find myself again. You gave me hope. It was exactly the gift I needed."

I seriously doubted I had done any of that, and if I had it was only because she was ready to be invited back into her own skin. However, I was willing to take credit where it wasn't due—being in showbiz had taught me that much.

"Does that mean you're feeling happier, these days?" I asked.

She smiled that melting, haunting smile of hers, only this time it was unclouded by sorrow. "I'm the happiest I've been since Daisy."

"People love you," I said. "I know it's not perfect, and I know it's not the same as having a partner, but it counts."

Layla put her arm around my waist. "I'm not ready for a partner. But I can see the time coming when I will be, and that's a wonderful feeling. Thank you for loving me even though it didn't take the form you wanted."

"Well, you can't always get what you want." I kissed her cheek. "But, if the Fates are kind, sometimes you get what you need."

I had wanted Layla. But I needed Luke.

And now, in the garden at my parent's place, we're getting married, and the people I love most on this earth are waiting for me. Mom and Dad. Suzie. Layla and Eric. Peaches, Bella, and Siren.

Mr. Goldman is here. He brought his mom. My Aunt Shirley didn't come because we're gay and she hates that yet another of her Satanic predictions came true—I found true love in a place of depravity and loud music.

Tiggy isn't happy, but she's organized the kind of saturation media that Ellen and Anne Heche never got, even for their breakup. She polled fans at some of our sites and says the overwhelming consensus is that everyone hates the marriage idea, and hates me, because they're fixated on Luke. Apparently, after all this, I still flunk the charisma test.

I set out two years ago to become a different person and in the end, I'm still myself. One thing has changed, though. I now know who that person is, and I like her.

About the Author

Grace Lennox is a pen name of best-selling lesbian author Jennifer Fulton. The author lives in the Midwest with her partner and animal companions. Her vice of choice is writing; however, she is also devoted to her wonderful daughter and her hobbies—fly fishing, cinema, and fine cooking. Grace started writing stories almost as soon as she could read them, and never stopped. Under pen names Grace Lennox, Jennifer Fulton, and Rose Beecham, she has published twelve novels and a handful of short stories.

Look for information about her work at www.boldstrokesbooks.com.

Books Available From Bold Strokes Books

Chance by Grace Lennox. At twenty-six, Chance Delaney decides her life isn't working so she swaps it for a different one. What follows is the sexy, funny, touching story of two women who, in finding themselves, also find one another. (1-933110-31-7)

The Exile and the Sorcerer by Jane Fletcher. First in the Lyremouth Chronicles. Tevi, wounded and adrift, arrives in the courtyard of a shy young sorcerer. Together they face monsters, magic, and the challenge of loving despite their differences. (1-933110-32-5)

A Matter of Trust by Radclyffe. JT Sloan is a cybersleuth who doesn't like attachments. Michael Lassiter is leaving her husband, and she needs Sloan's expertise to safeguard her company. It should just be business—but it turns into much more. (1-933110-33-3)

Sweet Creek by Lee Lynch. A celebration of the enduring nature of love, friendship, and community in the quirky, heart-warming lesbian community of Waterfall Falls. (1-933110-29-5)

The Devil Inside by Ali Vali. Derby Cain Casey, head of a New Orleans crime organization, runs the family business with guts and grit, and no one crosses her. No one, that is, until Emma Verde claims her heart and turns her world upside down. (1-933110-30-9)

Grave Silence by Rose Beecham. Detective Jude Devine's investigation of a series of ritual murders is complicated by her torrid affair with the golden girl of Southwestern forensic pathology, Dr. Mercy Westmoreland. (1-933110-25-2)

Honor Reclaimed by Radclyffe. In the aftermath of 9/11, Secret Service Agent Cameron Roberts and Blair Powell close ranks with a trusted few to find the would-be assassins who nearly claimed Blair's life. (1-933110-18-X)

Honor Bound by Radclyffe. Secret Service Agent Cameron Roberts and Blair Powell face political intrigue, a clandestine threat to Blair's safety, and the seemingly irreconcilable personal differences that force them ever farther apart. (1-933110-20-1)

Protector of the Realm: Supreme Constellations Book One by Gun Brooke. A space adventure filled with suspense and a daring intergalactic romance featuring Commodore Rae Jacelon and a stunning, but decidedly lethal, Kellen O'Dal. (1-933110-26-0)

Innocent Hearts by Radclyffe. In a wild and unforgiving land, two women learn about love, passion, and the wonders of the heart. (1-933110-21-X)

The Temple at Landfall by Jane Fletcher. An imprinter, one of Celaeno's most revered servants of the Goddess, is also a prisoner to the faith—until a Ranger frees her by claiming her heart. The Celaeno series. (1-933110-27-9)

Force of Nature by Kim Baldwin. From tornados to forest fires, the forces of nature conspire to bring Gable McCoy and Erin Richards close to danger, and closer to each other. (1-933110-23-6)

In Too Deep by Ronica Black. Undercover homicide cop Erin McKenzie tracks a femme fatale who just might be a real killer…with love and danger hot on her heels. (1-933110-17-1)

Stolen Moments: *Erotic Interludes 2* by Stacia Seaman and Radclyffe, eds. Love on the run, in the office, in the shadows…Fast, furious, and almost too hot to handle. (1-933110-16-3)

Course of Action by Gun Brooke. Actress Carolyn Black desperately wants the starring role in an upcoming film produced by Annelie Peterson. Just how far will she go for the dream part of a lifetime? (1-933110-22-8)

Rangers at Roadsend by Jane Fletcher. Sergeant Chip Coppelli has learned to spot trouble coming, and that is exactly what she sees in her new recruit, Katryn Nagata. The Celaeno series. (1-933110-28-7)

Justice Served by Radclyffe. Lieutenant Rebecca Frye and her lover, Dr. Catherine Rawlings, embark on a deadly game of hide-and-seek with an underworld kingpin who traffics in human souls. (1-933110-15-5)

Distant Shores, Silent Thunder by Radclyffe. Doctor Tory King—and the women who love her—is forced to examine the boundaries of love, friendship, and the ties that transcend time. (1-933110-08-2)

Hunter's Pursuit by Kim Baldwin. A raging blizzard, a mountain hideaway, and a killer-for-hire set a scene for disaster—or desire—when Katarzyna Demetrious rescues a beautiful stranger. (1-933110-09-0)

The Walls of Westernfort by Jane Fletcher. All Temple Guard Natasha Ionadis wants is to serve the Goddess—until she falls in love with one of the rebels she is sworn to destroy. The Celaeno series. (1-933110-24-4)

Change Of Pace: *Erotic Interludes* by Radclyffe. Twenty-five hot-wired encounters guaranteed to spark more than just your imagination. Erotica as you've always dreamed of it. (1-933110-07-4)

Honor Guards by Radclyffe. In a wild flight for their lives, the president's daughter and those who are sworn to protect her wage a desperate struggle for survival. (1-933110-01-5)

Fated Love by Radclyffe. Amidst the chaos and drama of a busy emergency room, two women must contend not only with the fragile nature of life, but also with the irresistible forces of fate. (1-933110-05-8)

Justice in the Shadows by Radclyffe. In a shadow world of secrets and lies, Detective Sergeant Rebecca Frye and her lover, Dr. Catherine Rawlings, join forces in the elusive search for justice. (1-933110-03-1)

shadowland by Radclyffe. In a world on the far edge of desire, two women are drawn together by power, passion, and dark pleasures. An erotic romance. (1-933110-11-2)

Love's Masquerade by Radclyffe. Plunged into the indistinguishable realms of fiction, fantasy, and hidden desires, Auden Frost is forced to question all she believes about the nature of love. (1-933110-14-7)

Love & Honor by Radclyffe. The president's daughter and her lover are faced with difficult choices as they battle a tangled web of Washington intrigue for...love and honor. (1-933110-10-4)

Beyond the Breakwater by Radclyffe. One Provincetown summer three women learn the true meaning of love, friendship, and family. (1-933110-06-6)

Tomorrow's Promise by Radclyffe. One timeless summer, two very different women discover the power of passion to heal and the promise of hope that only love can bestow. (1-933110-12-0)

Love's Tender Warriors by Radclyffe. Two women who have accepted loneliness as a way of life learn that love is worth fighting for and a battle they cannot afford to lose. (1-933110-02-3)

Love's Melody Lost by Radclyffe. A secretive artist with a haunted past and a young woman escaping a life that has proved to be a lie find their destinies entwined. (1-933110-00-7)

Safe Harbor by Radclyffe. A mysterious newcomer, a reclusive doctor, and a troubled gay teenager learn about love, friendship, and trust during one tumultuous summer in Provincetown. (1-933110-13-9)

Above All, Honor by Radclyffe. Secret Service Agent Cameron Roberts fights her desire for the one woman she can't have—Blair Powell, the daughter of the president of the United States. (1-933110-04-X)